"He's mine, isn't he?"

"Yes."

Nick rolled over on his back. Patrick was *his* son.

No wonder he'd liked the boy so much. Damn, he was a bright kid. Good-looking, too. He'd be a heart-breaker, that's for sure. Just like his dad.

He was a father. He had a child with Jenny, who meant more to him than any woman, any person, ever had.

He rolled back to his side and found Jenny staring at him with wide, frightened eyes. He touched her cheek, lifted a tear with his index finger. "We have a kid," he whispered. "How do you like that?"

"I like it fine. How about you?"

"I'm knocked out," he said. "Patrick's an amazing kid. And you. You're…"

"I'm what?"

Reality set in just then, and his mood darkened. "In danger. We have to get the hell out of here before we're caught, before they know the truth…."

Dear Harlequin Intrigue Reader,

Spring is in the air and we have a month of fabulous books for you to curl up with as the March winds howl outside:

- Familiar is back on the prowl, in Caroline Burnes's *Familiar Texas*. And *Rocky Mountain Maneuvers* marks the conclusion of Cassie Miles's COLORADO CRIME CONSULTANTS trilogy.

- Jessica Andersen brings us an exciting medical thriller, *Covert M.D.*

- Don't miss the next ECLIPSE title, Lisa Childs's *The Substitute Sister*.

- Definitely check out our April lineup. Debra Webb is starting THE ENFORCERS, an exciting new miniseries you won't want to miss. Also look for a special 3-in-1 story from Rebecca York, Ann Voss Peterson and Patricia Rosemoor called *Desert Sons*.

Each month, Harlequin Intrigue brings you a variety of heart-stopping romantic suspense and chilling mystery. Don't miss a single book!

Sincerely,

Denise O'Sullivan
Senior Editor
Harlequin Intrigue

NOT-SO-SECRET BABY

JO LEIGH

HARLEQUIN®

TORONTO • NEW YORK • LONDON
AMSTERDAM • PARIS • SYDNEY • HAMBURG
STOCKHOLM • ATHENS • TOKYO • MILAN • MADRID
PRAGUE • WARSAW • BUDAPEST • AUCKLAND

ISBN 0-373-22835-X

NOT-SO-SECRET BABY

Printed in U.S.A.

ABOUT THE AUTHOR

Jo Leigh lives way the heck up on a mountain in Utah with her own personal hero and her many chipmunk friends. She loves to hear from readers at http://www.joleigh.com.

Books by Jo Leigh

CAST OF CHARACTERS

Jenny Granger—She escaped from a madman once, but now he has her baby!

Nick Mason—With the world's safety at stake, how can he blow his cover and help the woman he loves?

Patrick Granger—Two and a half; the innocent child born in secret.

C. Randall Todd—Casino mogul, billionaire, killer.

Henry Sweet—Todd's right-hand man, with an itch to get rid of Nick Mason.

Chapter One

Once the coast was clear, Jeannie hurried over to where Kelly was picking up the Lincoln Logs. "Tanya called me this morning," she said, keeping her voice low so none of the other mommies could hear. "Her Nate got a call yesterday to fix an air conditioner at Mary Pierson's place. He said she's just as neat as a pin. Nothing out of place, not even in the baby's room. He said she's got one of those leather couches they were selling at The Junction last summer. You know, the leather seconds? And she's got a ton of books lining the walls in the living room."

Kelly dumped an armload of pieces into the big cardboard box. "Did he see her bedroom?"

Jeannie nodded. "Double bed. Dresser. An armoire he swears used to belong to Ann Keating before her husband died."

"I remember that. She had that garage sale. I picked up her old stand mixer. It still works. I made up a batch of butter cookies for the church bazaar just last month."

"Oh, yeah. They were scrumptious. But here's the

thing," Jeannie continued. "Nate said she didn't have any pictures except two of baby Patrick. Nothing on the mantel, nothing in the bedroom. It's like the woman has no past. Like she came here from outer space or something."

"My Alan, he says she never talks about herself at work. He says she reads on break or she writes in that journal of hers. Lisa asked her straight-out where Patrick's daddy was and she wouldn't say. She said she didn't like to talk about it. If you want my opinion, I'm thinking he was bad news, you know? Hit her, probably. Like Bonnie's husband?"

"That, or she doesn't know who the daddy is." Jeannie bent to pick up a Barbie doll. "She has that sadness about her. So pretty, and yet, I don't know…"

"Yeah," Kelly said. "Like she's running from something."

"Heck, why else would a single woman move to Milford? She has no family here."

"I remember the day she got here. She was driving that beat-up old Chevy."

"Still is."

"Right."

"How long has it been?"

"Got to be two years."

Jeannie nodded. "Two years, and we still don't know beans about her."

"Not that she isn't nice."

Jeannie shook her head, a strand of auburn hair loosening from under her headband. "Nice as can be for someone with so many secrets. Lily, you put that down right now."

Kelly glanced over at Lily, Jeannie's three-year-old who'd gotten hold of the watercolor paint set. Kelly's son, Jack, had been born two weeks to the day of Lily's birth, sealing their already solid friendship. "I surely would like to know what happened to that girl."

"Me, too." Jeannie shook her head. "Maybe I'll do a little research at the library, now that they've got the Internet."

"Oh, good idea. Why don't we go tomorrow?"

"Can't. I have a doctor's appointment."

"How about Friday?"

"Friday. Okay. We'll take the kids."

MARY PIERSON walked down Hill Street toward the market, her young son holding her hand, scurrying on his short legs to keep up. Mary let him step on the mat in front of the grocery store so that the automatic doors would open. He liked that.

Inside, Gary, the butcher, waved. "Getting ready to close shop here. You gonna need anything? I could cut it fresh for you."

"No, thanks," Mary told him. "Just grabbing a few things."

"Okay. Next time."

"Next time." She put Patrick in the cart seat and headed down the aisle. Canned corn, tomato soup, bread, milk, butter. She picked through the skimpy produce selection, finally choosing a reasonably fresh head of lettuce and some broccoli. She chose a prewrapped pound of hamburger and, on her way to the register, added a package of spaghetti. Patrick loved spaghetti.

"How are you this evening, Mary?"

"Fine, Marge. You?" Mary lifted her boy from the cart while Marge toted up the groceries and placed them on the belt.

"I'm good, thanks."

Mary could see the older woman wanted to talk, but it was late and all she wanted was to get home. "Could you toss in a book of stamps, please?"

"Sure, Mary. Sure."

"Thanks." Mary smiled, then turned her attention to Patrick pulling on her arm. "Hang tight, soldier. We'll be done here soon."

Patrick tugged harder. "I'm hungry."

"I know, baby. Soon."

"That's twelve twenty-five," Marge said.

Mary paid in cash, as always.

"Wait a second."

Grabbing her bags, Mary looked back at the checker.

Marge leaned over the counter, holding a red lollipop down to Patrick. "It's okay, isn't it, Mary?"

"Of course. What do you say, Patrick?"

"Thank you."

"Well, you're welcome, honey."

"Thanks, again," Mary said, ushering Patrick toward the door. Mary felt her shoulders relax the moment they were outside.

Patrick chattered the whole way home, which wasn't

very far. After she parked, she took him out of his car seat and handed him the can of tomato soup. He hurried toward their front door, proud to be helping with the groceries. She watched him run up the short path, his blond hair flopping around his ears, his jeans just like the big kids wore. She loved him so much it ached.

Mary'd been looking forward to making a nice meal for the two of them. Not that she didn't cook every day, but she had Friday and Saturday off from her waitressing job at the Hong Kong Café. That meant she could spend some extra time on dinner, make chocolate pudding for dessert. After, they'd watch a movie, probably *The Wizard of Oz,* Patrick's new favorite. After Patrick went to bed, she intended to soak in a hot tub. Scented candles, lavender bath salts and the new Patricia Cornwall novel. Heaven.

"Mommy, come on!"

"Hold your horses," she said, grabbing the bag of groceries from the trunk of her old Chevy. "I'm coming."

By the time she got to the door, Patrick had forgotten the can of soup, left squarely in the center of the doormat, and had turned his attention to the wind chimes hanging from a small branch of the elm tree that shaded the front of the house. He couldn't quite reach the silver tubes, but he was growing so fast, it wouldn't be a problem for long.

She cradled the grocery bag on her hip as she opened the door. As soon as the lock clicked, Patrick pushed ahead of her and raced inside. His energy amazed her. Her own energy level continued to dwindle. She knew the reason and wished she could do something about it, but… It might do her some good to start her new craft project—making bath salts and selling them at the local flea market. She'd never been a particularly craft-wise person, but there were only so many books one could read, so much time she could focus on her son.

She closed the door behind her, locking both dead bolts. A quick glance at the windows and around the living room showed her nothing had been disturbed.

"Cookie?"

Patrick, at two and a half, was her own personal cookie monster, with chocolate chip being the uncontested favorite. She'd had to put them up on top of the fridge and dole them out or he'd just munch through the whole batch in one sitting. "Yes, but only after we put away the groceries."

"Okay." With that, he was off like a shot, waiting in the middle of the kitchen for her to get her act in gear. She smiled, even while she had to chase away thoughts of what Patrick's life should have been. No use going there. This was a good life, a safe life, and that was all that mattered.

Thank heaven for the activities at the library. And, of course, Alice, who watched Patrick five days a week. Mary sighed. She really should try to make friends with the other mothers in town. She just wasn't ready. Not yet.

She lifted the bag to the counter. Patrick could put the bread in the breadbox. He had to drag over the little stool, but once situated, he did the job like a fine young man. She, meanwhile, put the milk and butter in the fridge, then pulled out the hamburger for tonight's spaghetti.

"Now?"

She looked down. Patrick had put the stool away and stood staring up at her, his blue eyes eager, his body bouncing with anticipation.

"Yes, now."

He thrust his hands up in the air as if he'd just scored the winning touchdown. She reached up and grabbed the cookie jar, then gave him his prize. "Would you like milk or juice?"

"Juice."

She put the cookies back and took a juice box from the fridge. He was already at the table, his legs swinging back and forth, his cookie the only thing in the world.

She'd make up a batch of bath salts tonight. Use it herself to see if she liked the fragrance.

So it wasn't a thrill a minute. So what? It was safe. Safe was good.

SHE WOKE with a start, a sudden swell of panic in her stomach, a tightening in her chest. For a moment she held her breath, didn't move an inch, just listened. There was the tick of the clock on her nightstand. Behind that, the quiet of Milford at four in the morning. But the silence did little to assuage her anxiety.

She threw back her comforter, put her legs over the side of the bed and slipped on her pale yellow slippers. Her robe, the one she'd bought from the Sears catalog, was perched at the ready on a hook by the door. She was halfway to Patrick's room before she tied it on.

With each step the dread and fear worsened, all her nightmares of the past two and a half years melding together into an unthinkable terror. This wasn't like the other nights she'd awakened from a bad dream... Her baby. Something...someone...

She flew into his room and the unthinkable became reality.

Patrick was gone.

She called out, but only once. Then her throat closed and the blood in her veins turned to ice. The window—his window, with the locks and the safety glass—open. His quilt on the floor, his Spider-Man sheet balled up, tossed aside. His pillow still held the impression of his head. So small.

And, in the middle of the bed, an envelope. Her hand shook so hard she could hardly pick it up.

When she finally did, it was a note telling her when to be at the Cedar City airport. It wasn't signed. But then, it didn't have to be.

THE VEGAS STRIP tried to be glamorous during the day, but it didn't succeed. Like an aging actress without her makeup, all the flaws came to the fore in sunlight. The sun-baked sidewalks, the desperate bids from the small casinos, begging gamblers to come for the ninety-nine-cent, foot-long hot dogs and stay for the video poker.

Nick Mason hated the place. Hated the thousands of lights, the electronic billboards with the perfect pictures and snazzy ads. He hated the heat of the place, which, according to the morning news, was almost one hundred, and it wasn't even nine. If he'd had his way, he'd live in the mountains. Aspen, maybe, or Boulder. Somewhere green with thick trees and lots of water. He'd have himself a nice little cabin that had no address. Where he could walk to the nearest stream to catch his dinner.

This town wasn't real. Yeah, okay, so there was Henderson and Summerlin, where there were grocery stores and dry cleaners, but there were poker machines in every damn market, in every gas station, in every drugstore. The ubiquitous machines lent an air of desperation to the most mundane of tasks. Just ask the housewife who spent five hundred bucks on that gallon of milk. Or the bank teller who'd lost the rent…again.

He'd been here too long, that was the problem. Living a nighttime life. If you were a player in Vegas, you slept during the day. Nothing important ever happened before sundown. Which could help explain his crappy attitude. He'd gotten to bed after four this morning, then Todd had called to tell him to make a pickup at the Henderson Executive Airport.

Normally he wouldn't have to do anything so plebian, but Todd's driver had gotten some bad sushi at one of those $3.99 buffets downtown and was riding it out at the Sunrise Hospital. As always, Nick had said, "Yes, sir," keeping his voice even and his attitude go-to. Playing the part as if his life depended on it. Which it did.

He'd started working for C. Randall Todd three years

ago. It had taken him all that time to gain a position of
trust in the organization. Everybody who worked for
Todd had to prove themselves worthy. The tests weren't
for the weak. Despite the fact that Todd's business prac-
tices were impressive enough to pass the rigors of the
Nevada Gaming Commission regulations, the man himself was a throwback to the old Vegas. No one double-
crossed Todd. Not twice, at least.

Nick himself had done his time as Todd's hatchet
man. No one had ever ended up dead, but they'd been
hurt something wicked. It turned his stomach to think
about it, so he didn't. Simple.

Enough. He had to get showered, put something in
his stomach and get down to the airport on time. He
threw the covers aside and hit the floor for his push-ups.
One hundred. Every morning. No exceptions.

When he finished counting, he headed for the bathroom. Part of his incentive for completing his push-ups
in good time was this little trick: no john until he was
through. Some days were easier than others.

As he went through the rest of his morning routine,
he wondered who was coming in. Todd hadn't told him
and he hadn't asked. But it must be a hell of a whale to
call out the boss's private limo.

He remembered the first time he'd heard talk about
whales. It was his second week in Vegas and he was so
green he disappeared in front of the MGM Grand.
Sweet, Todd's majordomo, had been talking about this
whale and that whale, and it had been everything Nick
could do not to ask what the hell was going on. That

night he'd done some research and discovered that "whale" was the designated slang for a high roller. A really high roller.

The minimum they had to bank was five million, at least at Todd's hotel. Granted, Xanadu was as ritzy as it got in Vegas, but most of the major hotels had similar limits. Whales cost big money. But there was one basic fact about Las Vegas: casinos were not in the business of making gamblers rich. Anyone who thought different ought to check out the trailer parks on Main. Most of the decrepit mobile homes had doors. Some had windows. Not many.

Whales, on the other hand, had money to burn. At least, that's how they acted when they came to his turf. It was like something out of an old Russian novel how these people got treated. It started with the private jet, the limo, the personal butler, the multimillion-dollar private suite complete with grand piano, twenty-four-hour massage service, personal swimming pool, personal chef. The list went on and on. If one of Todd's whales wanted a purple elephant, he'd get one.

But there were whales and there were whales. This one, the one coming in at noon, had to be a mark in the billions, because Todd was stingy with his toys. Xanadu had a fleet of ten stretch limos for the customers. Todd's personal limo put them all to shame.

Personally, Nick hated driving the monstrosity. It was huge, longer than a normal stretch, and white. Inside and out. He especially hated the button in the back that let the passenger speak to the driver. The reverb crap on the mike altered the sound so it sounded like the voice of God telling the peon behind the wheel to stop at the Indian smoke shop to pick up cigarettes.

He was, of course, expected to act like Jeeves, which unfortunately wasn't that much of a stretch from how he was expected to act around the boss. Although Todd wasn't particularly hung up on the words. "Sir" was good, but not essential. "Very good, sir," was over-the-top. The important thing to Todd was that when he said jump, his employees already knew how high. Todd didn't give second chances.

Nick put on his lightweight black suit, the one that made him look more like a mortician than a chauffeur. His shirt was silk, the tie Hermès. When you worked for C. Randall Todd, you dressed the part.

He took a final look in the mirror, satisfied that he would pass muster, then he headed out. He lived on the fortieth floor of the hotel, the floor below the really expensive suites. It had taken getting used to, living in a place like this, but it had its advantages. Housekeeping was one. He just had to make sure he put everything important in his room safe. There was no doubt in his mind that Todd had the staff search the rooms on a regular basis. Paranoia was the word of the year around Xanadu, and Nick was just as guilty as anyone else. Todd's basic belief was that everyone was out to get him, including his own family. Probably why he was as successful as he was.

The man was worth billions. And not only from his gaming and hotel interests. He was also incredibly powerful in the military surveillance business. That little sideline had begun fifteen years ago, when Todd's first hotel had hosted an arms show.

The El Rio had been his maiden venture into the world of Vegas, but the relatively small hotel had outlived its usefulness and was scheduled for destruction. As with everything else in Sin City, the event was being made into a spectacle. Like the Dunes, the Sands and the original Aladdin, the El Rio was going to be imploded. On the Fourth of July, no less.

In its place, Todd planned another luxury hotel, this one smaller but even more exclusive than the Xanadu. It would make the Belagio look like a Motel 6.

Nick got to the elevator and pressed the button, his gaze moving from the ornate flower arrangements on the antique tables to the mirrors on the walls. He did look as though he was about to get into a hearse. At least he wasn't required to wear a damn hat.

The elevator doors opened and he got in, expecting a long, slow ride down. There were express elevators in the hotel, but not from his floor. He amused himself by counting the stops on the way to the lobby. Six. He always left about ten minutes early to accommodate.

Finally he reached the basement level. He'd go to the employee's lounge and grab something to eat. Then he'd be on his way. He wanted the airport run over quickly so he could get back. Todd had canceled one important meeting this afternoon with Steve Wynn, but he hadn't canceled his appointment with Rafe Shaharid, one of his major customers. Everything about the meeting was legal, at least on the surface. But Nick had a feeling there was something more going on.

He had no intention of being left out of the loop on this one. It could be big. Real big.

NICK PARKED THE LIMO on the tarmac and got out. Todd's Gulfstream IV was already here, just shutting down. Nick straightened his jacket and waited for the passenger to disembark.

The jet door opened and the attendant stepped out first. Gina was her name, and she was as beautiful as any of the showgirls at the hotel. She was a favorite of Todd's and Nick knew for a fact that she offered more than coffee and tea whenever the boss was on board.

Another woman stepped onto the platform and Nick stopped breathing.

What in hell was she doing back?

Chapter Two

Nick pulled himself together as it registered that it really was Jenny. He would have known her anywhere. God, how many times had he thought he'd seen her in a restaurant or at a gas station? How many nights had she haunted his dreams…?

She'd come back. If he hadn't seen her with his own eyes, he'd never have believed it.

She walked down the metal ladder to the tarmac, a purse over her shoulder, an overnight case in her hand. She had her hair pulled back in a ponytail, as if she'd thrown it up in a hurry. Sunglasses hid her eyes, but the thin line of her lips telegraphed her anxiety.

His gaze moved down the rest of her, the long, slender body he'd known too briefly. She seemed awfully thin, fragile. He'd always thought of her as fragile, though.

Her jeans were worn Levi's, her shirt plain white, short-sleeved, pressed. None of the designer clothes she'd worn when he'd known her before. Why in hell was she back? Surely she wasn't going to hook up with Todd again. Hadn't she had enough?

He remembered the last time he'd seen her. She'd been scared. No, terrified. As he had with every other possession, Todd had held on to her with an iron fist. She'd had to plan an escape, as daring as any prison break. Like a fool, Nick had helped her, putting everything he had on the line. He should have stayed out of it. But the welts on her back, the bruises on her legs...

She said something to Gina, then turned his way, walked as if each step cost her, which, if she was headed back to the Xanadu, was sickeningly true.

He opened the back door of the limo, took his place beside it. Waited as she got closer. Wondered...

She stopped about twenty-five yards from the car. Her mouth opened slightly as she recognized him. With a slow hand, she took off her dark sunglasses.

Where she'd looked anxious a moment ago, he now saw surprise furrow her brow. She hadn't expected him. Was she pleased? Embarrassed?

Moving forward again, her gaze moved down to the tarmac until she was even with the front of the limo. "Nick," she said, her voice bringing back memories he'd just as soon forget.

"I never expected to see you again."

She closed her eyes briefly and when she opened them again he saw a hardness that hadn't been there the last time he'd seen her. "Things change."

"Yeah," he said. He took her overnight bag, like the good little chauffeur that he was, then helped her into the cavernous back seat, startled at how she nearly disappeared against the white of the interior.

He put her bag in the trunk, then got in behind the wheel. The moment he turned on the engine, the bullet-proof Plexiglas that separated the wheat from the chaff lowered a few inches. Not enough for him to see more than the top of her pale blond head, but enough for him to hear her.

"How have you been?" she asked.

"Me? Swell. In fact, I haven't had to be a driver for over a year, with the obvious exception of this trip. I'm moving up the food chain."

"I see," she said, although he knew she didn't see at all.

"What brings you back to sunny Las Vegas? Come to see the new Celine Dion theater?"

She didn't answer until he'd reached St. Rose Parkway, heading toward 15. "I see you've still got that charming wit."

He glanced in the rearview, but she was staring out her window, hidden once more behind her sunglasses. "I just do what I'm told," he said. "Keep my nose clean."

He heard her sigh, and for a moment he felt bad. But only for a moment. She'd gotten away once. He doubted she'd get away again. The woman knew who Todd was, had seen what he could do. And still, she'd come back. Probably for the money. Wasn't that always the bottom line?

Hell, she'd never had it so good as when she belonged to Todd. She'd been a cocktail waitress working her way through U.N.L.V. when Todd had found her. He'd fallen hard from the first moment he'd laid eyes on her and he'd pursued her with his unique brand of determination. Jenny had been all of twenty-one when he'd begun his campaign. Todd'd treated her like a queen, taking her to the best shows, the finest restaurants. They'd traveled a lot in the jet and he'd even set her up with her own suite at Xanadu. Right down the hall from his.

Nick had been an errand boy back then. He'd just started with the organization and was learning the ropes when he'd been assigned as her driver and bodyguard.

Nick had been attracted to her from the start. Who wouldn't be? It wasn't just her looks, although they would have been enough, but Jenny was bright, funny and had a sweetness about her that made him think of his childhood in Wichita. Todd had him watch her like a hawk, not the least bit afraid that Nick would take advantage of the situation. A man would have to be an idiot to touch Todd's woman.

But during that time Nick had come to know her. He'd understood how she'd found herself in a situation she'd been woefully unprepared to handle. By the time she'd figured it all out, it had been too late. A captive in a glitter palace, she was subject to Todd's capriciousness and vile temper. That's why Nick had helped her. Because she'd been a victim. This time, she was walking in of her own free will. She probably thought she had good reasons, but as far as he could tell, no reason could be good enough for someone like Jenny to walk back into the lion's den.

A soft mechanical whir made him look back just in time to see the window go up, locking them each in their own compartments. He wished she would move so he could see her more clearly in the rearview. But maybe she didn't want to be seen.

He kept his eyes on the road. She wasn't his affair. Messing with Jenny Granger was a surefire way to get himself killed.

JENNY LEANED HER HEAD back against the plush white leather of the limo seat. She knew Todd wouldn't hurt Patrick, but the knowledge didn't make things easier. There were only three things she loved in this whole world. Her mother. Her son. And the man in the front seat.

At least, she'd thought she'd loved him.

She stared out the window at the familiar landscape. Here, in Henderson, the city looked like any other. There was the Super Kmart, the 99-Cent store, the dry cleaner's. Of course, other cities didn't have casinos every few blocks or video poker in the grocery stores. But lives were led here that weren't connected to the massive gaming industry. Kids went to school, mothers drove in car pools.

She hadn't seen her own mother in more than two years. Like someone in the Witness Security Program, she'd cut off her ties to the past, because she'd known Todd would stop at nothing to find her. She still couldn't figure out how her cover had been blown. She'd been meticulous in her deception, covering every base. She had a birth certificate and social security card, both in the name of Mary Pierson. She'd moved to Milford knowing Todd had never heard of the place and that she had no ties to the tiny city whatsoever.

So where had she slipped up? She shook her head. What difference did it make? He'd found her. Discovered Patrick. And now, she was sure, he'd demand his pound of flesh.

She'd done the one thing Todd couldn't tolerate—she'd tricked him. She'd run off with no warning and no word. Risked everything. He hadn't known she was pregnant. But he had decided to marry her. In those last few weeks, she'd been witness to Todd's astonishing ego, his taste for luxury and glitz.

No one belonged in Las Vegas more than C. Randall Todd. He was the epitome of conspicuous consumption, and for Todd more was not enough. Nothing was enough. God, the money he'd spent on her. She could have lived for a year in Milford on the diamond he'd given her for their first month anniversary. If she'd taken it with her. She hadn't. She hadn't wanted anything of his, no matter how high the resale value. He was the most purely evil man she'd ever met.

Stupid, stupid and naive. She'd never believed anyone could be that evil, not in the flesh. She'd been so blind, so trusting. There was no one to blame but herself, and now Patrick was in the bastard's clutches.

She would not cry. Her gaze moved back to the man behind the wheel. Big mistake.

Nick Mason. The one bright light in what had been the worst year of her life. Yes, he'd been a part of Todd's machine, but he wasn't like the others. Not like Henry Sweet, Todd's right-hand man who frightened her almost as much as Todd himself. No, Nick had been human toward her, even kind. For a long time she'd even thought he'd felt more. It didn't matter. He'd helped her escape despite the terrible risk.

She'd tried to convince him to leave, too, but he'd been stubborn. Adamant that staying with Todd would ensure his future, even though he knew the kind of man Todd was. But he'd clearly succumbed to Todd's philosophy: get what you want, no matter who it hurt or what it cost. The moment she'd seen Nick's face she realized whatever tenderness he'd felt for her had evolved into something bitter and harsh. What she hadn't counted on was how much that realization would hurt.

He must know that Todd had Patrick. How could he possibly be a part of that? She yearned to ask him about it, to find out if her boy was okay, but she knew better. The limo was undoubtedly bugged. Todd never let an opportunity pass to trip someone up. If she said the wrong thing, it could cost her more than she could afford.

Clearly the years had not been kind to Nick, at least on the inside. The facade had held up, though. Time hadn't changed the fact that he was the best-looking man she'd ever seen.

His dark hair was shorter, parted on the side, debonair with just a hint of gray at the temples. He had that damn cleft in his chin that had held her fascination for countless hours. He had thick, expressive eyebrows designed to bring attention to his amazing eyes. His body still made her think of tightly coiled strength, powerful beneath the silk shirt, the elegantly simple suit.

He'd worked his looks to his advantage, knowing he

projected the perfect image of a high-powered, sophisticated big wheel. Just as Xanadu was the most opulent hotel casino in Vegas, the people closest to the man had to look like a million bucks 24/7. The only time she'd seen Nick out of a designer suit was when he'd jogged in the morning. And when he'd lain naked in her bed.

She shifted her gaze, unwilling to think about that time. Even though the repercussions continued to reverberate, it was history. She'd cut herself off from any part of Todd's world long ago, and this nightmare didn't change anything. She'd find a way to escape again. And to take her boy with her.

Looking down, it occurred to her that she wouldn't be wearing her jeans again, not while she was here. Todd had always wanted her to be as elegantly dressed as his staff. More so. It had taken her too long to understand that one of the reasons he hadn't wanted to let her go was that she looked like a cross between a showgirl and a schoolteacher. She'd been every bit as much a showpiece as the diamonds and the designer gowns he'd had her wear.

She caught Nick's gaze in the rearview mirror. He'd donned sunglasses, but his expression was hard as stone. Why? What had she done to him? More to the point, what kind of a horror story had Todd concocted to taint her?

She'd been so sure that beneath Nick's facade beat a good heart; held that notion close through almost three long years of isolation and strain. But now that she'd seen him again, she knew it had all been smoke and mirrors. She didn't really love him. She'd just built an elaborate fantasy out of loneliness and fear. Unfortunately, knowing that didn't make her feel any better.

She not only ached with worry for her baby, but the slender thread of hope that she'd have someone on her side had snapped when she'd first seen Nick. She was on her own. Which would have been okay if it hadn't been for Patrick. What kind of life would he have under the wing of such a vicious hawk?

Her eyes filled with hot tears and though she tried to blink them back, it was no use. Watching the Strip grow larger as they sped down the freeway turned the nightmare into reality.

Never before, not the whole time she'd been in Milford, had she felt so alone. Her wet gaze moved back to Nick, to his tense shoulders, his hand gripping the steering wheel. All the way to Las Vegas she'd staved off hysteria by thinking about Nick. Once again, she'd proved to herself that she was nothing more than a naive fool. Wrong in the most fundamental ways. Hell, she'd been wrong since the day she'd first met C. Randall Todd. But even so, some prices were too high to pay.

She wiped her cheeks with the backs of her hands and prayed to a God she no longer believed in. She was heading to hell in a white chariot. Alone. Completely alone.

LOCATED BETWEEN the Flamingo and Balley's, Xanadu was more of a palace than a hotel. With more than three thousand rooms, seven world-class restaurants, one of the largest casinos on the Strip, and a reputation for customer satisfaction unparalleled in a city known for indulgence, Xanadu far exceeded anything Kubla Khan could have imagined.

The building itself was silver and in the bright June sunlight it seemed molten and fluid, which was exactly what Todd had wanted. Using the old Coleridge poem as his guide, Todd had built the stately pleasure dome, complete with sunless sea, more than a mile of meandering river through woods and dales, leading to the mystical caverns below, where designer shops were carved out of rock and the music of the dulcimer floated in the purified air. All of it skillfully, masterfully, designed to part guests from their money.

As the limo approached the porte cochere, Jenny's stomach clenched as the fear she'd been keeping at arm's length sunk into her very bones. She had to swallow hard to keep from being sick and it was only thoughts of Patrick that kept her from running.

The window separating her from Nick lowered as they moved into the valet lane. "No place like home, eh?"

His sarcasm was as bitter as the bile in the back of her throat. "You've certainly made it yours," she said, struggling to keep her voice cool. "You must be so proud."

He parked the limo on the far side of the entrance, near the private elevators for the high rollers, then turned back to look at her as if she were something he'd found on the bottom of his shoe. "I am. But then, I never said I wanted out."

The valet opened the back door. She shot a look at Nick. "You bastard." She got out, blasted by the furnace-like heat of desert sun. The hotel was busy, as always. Taxis waited like schoolchildren to be called into service by the costumed bellmen. Limos stretched long and private in their own lanes. The glass doors leading inside were huge and thick, double doors meant to keep the real world firmly outside.

Nick walked to her side, holding her overnight bag. She hadn't brought much with her. Makeup, pictures, vitamins. Everything else would be provided for, down to her bra and panties. Oh, God, she couldn't do it.

She had to. Patrick was up there, scared to death, wanting his mommy. They'd never been apart this long. She had to see him—now.

"Come on," Nick said, his hand on the small of her back.

The contact made her shiver as it always had. Her foolish body didn't know any better, but it would learn. She stepped forward quickly, breaking the contact. She wanted nothing to do with him.

He led her inside to the atrium, twenty stories high, capped by a blanket of mirrors and hanging crystal in a flash of glitter. The sound of the casino was muted here. In fact, one of the conditions for having slots in this hotel was that there were no bells and whistles. People threw away their money quietly in Xanadu.

They walked past gardens, gazebos, pergolas lush with foliage. It took a staff of more than a hundred people to maintain the gardens in Xanadu, and in all the time she'd spent here she'd never once seen a brown leaf.

The smell of the place brought back too much. Of

course, there were no unpleasant odors. The air, along with everything else, was strictly controlled, manipulated. There were no clocks anywhere, the sky inside was always blue in the perpetual daylight. There was no breach of the fantasy where any guest might catch an inadvertent glimpse.

She looked up as they crossed to the private elevators, built slightly behind the public facilities, and saw the hundreds of smoky-glass domes in the ceiling and along the walls. Domes that hid security cameras. No hotel was more carefully monitored. The security staff outnumbered the garden staff.

Nick called for an elevator. Once they were inside, he slipped a key into the slot that would allow them passage to the upper floors, to the suites for the whales and Todd's enclave. It felt like forever to climb the forty-one stories. All she could think of was holding Patrick. Keeping him safe.

When they finally reached the penthouse, Nick walked with her down the hallway, her boots sinking into the thick pile of the burgundy carpet. The theme continued even here in the lofty heights, with Chinese and Mongol influences in the wall sconces, the paintings and the wallpaper. She'd been awed the first time Todd had brought her here. No detail left unattended, everything had a beauty and a serenity meant to soothe and to comfort. It didn't work on her. All she could think about was the fact that she'd need a key to get into any of the elevators on this floor. A key he'd never give her.

They stopped at the double doors to Todd's suite. It

was, of course, the most extravagant room in the hotel. More than fifteen-thousand square feet, it was larger than a lot of the motels on the side streets of the city and more decadent than a rock star's dreams.

Nick knocked and the door opened. A butler she didn't recognize bowed slightly, took her bag from Nick, then led them into the dragon's lair.

Marble floors, glass walls, Picassos, Renoirs, antiques; there wasn't an inch of the suite that wasn't detailed and designed to be the best of the best. Six bedrooms, twelve baths, a private swimming pool, spa, massage room, grand piano, private dining room and kitchen. It made her physically ill.

But she kept her expression neutral as they neared the master bedroom. He was going to test her—punish her. It would be horrible, but she could take it. She had to take it.

Patrick.

At the door, the butler knocked, then she heard Todd's voice. She gripped her purse, stood straight, focused. Feeling Nick beside her should have been a comfort, damn it.

The butler led them inside, and then she saw him. Patrick. Sitting on the lap of the man who would own her. Todd's hair, thick and shockingly white, was immaculate, as was the suit on his tall, muscular frame. A devilishly handsome man, he hid his wickedness behind hypnotically beautiful blue eyes.

"Mommy!"

She tore her gaze from Todd and hurried forward, her

anxiety to hold her child stronger than any fear. Patrick squirmed, trying to escape. When he couldn't, he cried, screamed, his panic loud and shrill in the cavernous room.

She reached the bedside chair where Todd held her son. Just as she was about to fall to her knees and beg, Patrick escaped. He leaped into her arms where she hugged him tight, her tears falling unheeded, his tears fueling her hatred drop by drop.

She looked up briefly, long enough to see that Todd was watching her intently, so she turned. But then she could see Nick. Was that shock in his face? Surprise? Had he really not known that Todd had kidnapped her baby?

Their baby?

Chapter Three

Nick struggled to keep the surprise off his face. A kid?
It explained so much. She'd wanted to get away from
Todd for a long time before she'd actually made a move.
Subtle hints, questions. But then, she'd gotten panicked,
insistent. She'd come to him that night…

Nick took a deep, slow breath as the realization
washed over him. She'd come to him, to his bed, even
though it could have gotten them both killed. She'd
known then, had to. She was carrying Todd's child.
Damn it, what a fool he'd been. He'd thought…

It didn't matter. It was his own damn fault that he'd let
himself care about her, that he'd put everything in jeop-
ardy. So what if her reasons had been more complicated?

His gaze went to the boy. How had he gotten here?
Nick hadn't heard a word about it. Why not? Why
hadn't Todd filled him in? Sweet had clearly known, but
then, Sweet knew everything. Almost everything. He
hadn't known Nick had helped Jenny escape, or Nick
would have been a corpse a long time ago.

Where was he, anyway? Todd couldn't itch without

Sweet scratching, and yet, here was this tender reunion scene and Henry Sweet was nowhere to be seen.

This whole situation stunk. And with what was coming down, Nick had better get to the bottom of it damn fast.

"You look like hell."

Nick shifted his attention to Todd. It was like old times, the way the man looked at Jenny. Todd was made of granite, except when he was around her. Nick had never met anyone who could master his emotions like C. Randall Todd. It was one of the things that made him so dangerous. And yet as he sat there on the edge of his bed, his face showed his lust, his need, his anger. So vividly, Nick had to stop himself from grabbing Jenny and the kid and running like hell.

Had she really come back to this of her own volition? Impossible. Obviously, Todd had found her, found out about his son, and from that moment there wasn't a force on earth that could have stopped him from getting the boy.

Todd considered himself the ruler of all he surveyed. And what could be more important to a ruler than an heir to the empire?

Jenny stood, holding fiercely to her son. "What I look like is no concern of yours."

Todd smiled. Nick felt his blood chill. Damn it, what was she thinking? She knew better than to provoke him.

"Get out, Nick. But don't go far. You'll be helping Jenny move into her old suite."

"Yes, sir," he said. There was nothing else he could say. He glanced at Jenny, but her attention was fully on

Todd. It didn't matter. He had to go. Now. He was in no position to help her. Not today. Not at all.

Jenny was on her own.

SHE HEARD THE DOOR behind her open and close behind Nick. Her bravado faltered, badly. Todd's gaze was enough to put the fear of the devil in anyone, but she knew, she remembered too intensely, just who she was facing.

"When we met, I thought your impertinence was charming. That was a long time ago."

"I'm still me, Todd. That's something you can't change."

"No?" He rose. She'd forgotten just how formidable a man he was, as if her memories could only hold so much of him and no more. At six foot two, he was a little shorter than Nick, but his attitude made him seem huge. He'd kept trim, which didn't surprise her. He had a personal trainer, played tennis and golf, swam daily. He took pride in his body and, just like everything else of his, it had to be a little better, a little stronger. He looked years younger than fifty-eight, something he never tired of hearing.

"No. I wish I could have been more…forthright about leaving, but the fundamental reasons haven't changed at all. I don't want to be here, Todd. You can have anyone. Anyone at all."

"That's right. I can. And I want you."

He reached her side and it was all she could do to maintain her ground. She couldn't give in to her terror.

Not that he didn't already know she was quaking inside. But she didn't want Patrick to see. He was scared enough as it was.

"Mommy, I want to go home."

She kissed his pale forehead. "I know, sweetie. Me, too."

Todd smiled at the boy, showing off his even, white teeth. Perfect. Fake. "You are home. This is your new home, son."

"He's not—" Jenny stopped herself. She'd gone over it and over it since the moment Patrick had disappeared. She didn't dare tell Todd that Patrick wasn't his. He wouldn't believe her; he'd insist on proof. Once he discovered that Nick was Patrick's father, the two of them were dead. What she didn't know, and didn't dare find out, is if it would also mean Patrick's death. Unthinkable, but Todd was just vicious enough to do something that heinous.

"He doesn't understand," she said feebly.

"Then we'll help him understand, won't we?" Todd declared, reaching out with his long fingers.

She flinched, but he only touched the side of her cheek. She closed her eyes, held Patrick tighter.

"Before you arrived, I explained to Patrick that I'm his father. That we'll become very good friends. That he'll have the best of everything from this moment forward. The best tutors, the best toys. And you, Jenny, will pull yourself together." He looked her up and down, shaking his head as if her jeans were a personal affront. "You're back with me now."

She bit back a smart-ass retort. It wouldn't help things. God, the helplessness was like drowning. How could she take it? "I didn't bring any clothes."

"There are some in your suite, and we'll get more when the time comes." A moment passed with his gaze burning into hers. He arched a white brow, waiting.

"Yes, sir," she said, making sure her voice sounded small, weak.

"Good. Now, go with Nick and get settled. I've put the boy next door to you, along with his nanny. I'll expect you back here in an hour. Alone. We need to set some ground rules." He smiled at her, but not with the warmth he'd shown Patrick. This was a feral smile, filled with the cruelty she'd learned to dread. "And we have some unfinished business to take care of, yes?"

She bit her lower lip to stop it from trembling as she nodded.

He leaned down and kissed her cheek, his breath a combination of mint and cloves that resurrected more of her past. She'd tried so hard to forget. But some horrors are not forgotten, ever.

He patted Patrick on the head. "Go. You haven't much time. And, Jenny, I want your hair down."

She turned, too fast. His hand was jolted from Patrick's head. She'd pay for that sin, too.

NICK LEANED against the open door of the last suite on the private floor, next to a middle-aged woman he'd just met, waiting for Jenny and Patrick. The woman, Regina Norris, was a professional nanny, British, who, she'd just told him, had once taken care of William and Harry, when the princess had been alive. Of late, she'd overseen the three children of a British Lord, and had come to America after being lured by an unimaginable sum by C. Randall Todd. Nick was faintly surprised. He'd have figured Todd would find someone more malleable for the job of watching his heir. Someone, say, from an old European family, but then again, it was his only son. Never settle for anything but the best, that was Todd's credo.

She looked like a nice woman. Well-kempt, prim. Sort of a Maggie Smith type. He quelled the urge to tell her to get out before it was too late. Before she made a mistake that could cost her everything. It wasn't his business.

Unfortunately, Todd had made Jenny Nick's business once again. He'd had to hide his shock at being assigned to her. It had been a long time since his bodyguard days. But when Nick thought about the other close associates of Todd's, he couldn't come up with anyone he'd trust to watch her.

It wasn't a question of loyalty. No one on the inner circle would dare make an inappropriate move. It was about intelligence. His men weren't exactly geniuses when it came to thinking on their feet.

Independent thought wasn't conducive to slavish obedience. Which, Nick had learned early and well, could be faked. But this assignment wasn't going to work at all. Not just because of their past, which would have been enough, but because of his future. Unfortunately he couldn't approach Todd about either of his reasons. So he'd have to come up with something else. Something compelling enough to get him back to his old routine without sending up any red flags.

The only thing he could think of was to have Jenny insist that he go. It wasn't a solution he cared for. He couldn't tell her what he was doing, that would put her in too much danger. So he'd have to be a schmuck.

Damn. As if things for her weren't terrible enough. But what was his alternative? Things were coming to a head here and he couldn't afford to have it all blow up in his face. That would be very, very bad.

Todd's door opened and Nick pushed off the wall, straightening his cuffs as he watched Jenny walk into the hall. She held her son tight and he watched her soothe the boy, touch him, hug him. He wondered who was more comforted.

Jenny had a kid. A son who looked just like her. Would Patrick grow more like Todd as he got older?

Nick still had a hell of a lot to think about, to work out. That he hadn't known about Patrick or Jenny returning bothered him almost as much as Jenny's return itself. At least he understood why she hadn't rushed to tell him about her boy when he'd put her in the limo. She'd known he'd figure out the dates. That she had to have been pregnant when they'd gotten together.

Would it have stopped him from helping her? No. Would it have stopped him from making love to her? He had no idea. And he couldn't afford to think about it now. His personal life was so far away from a priority, it had its own zip code. He'd given all that up when he'd taken the job with Todd. Nothing mattered but the gig. Not even Jenny.

What did matter was that his place in the organization was still safe. That Todd still trusted him. Henry Sweet didn't, but then, he never had. Sweet didn't trust anyone except Todd. Period. It had taken too long, at too great a cost, for Nick to get this far. He couldn't blow it now.

"There's my boy," Mrs. Norris said, stepping out to meet Jenny.

Nick held himself back as Jenny and the nanny met, sized each other up. Jenny held on to Patrick as long as she could, but in the end, she had to let him go. Patrick, of course, didn't care for that at all, and he let out a wail that was at once piercing and pathetic. Which wasn't nearly as bad as the sudden silence that descended when the nanny closed the door.

Jenny looked inconsolable. Damn it to hell, he couldn't have consoled her if he'd wanted to.

"So you're back to being my watchdog, eh, Nick?"

She'd turned to him slowly, walked away from her son, her ponytail swaying behind her as if her pale green eyes weren't half-dead with sorrow.

"Looks like it." He accompanied her back up the long hallway, past Todd's suite, to the room they both knew well. He opened the door to her suite, pocketing the key before he let her inside. She brushed by him quickly, but he still caught a whiff of her perfume. His body reacted quickly, but he ignored it.

"My God," she said as she gazed around the room. It was half the size of Todd's, but that still meant it was enormous. He'd redecorated since she'd gone, taken the once vaguely Persian decor and run with it. Pillows on the floor, silk curtain swathes hanging from the ceiling, great overstuffed chaise longues and ornate tables festooned with antique hookahs and cast-iron figurines. It was beautiful in a way, but so unlike Jenny's character as to be laughable.

"It looks like something out of Scheherazade's nightmares."

Nick smirked. "You managed to come up with enough tales to keep your head on."

Jenny whirled around, took a step toward him, her eyes fierce, her hands fisted. "What is it with you?" she said in a whisper that carried just to his ears and not the microphones studded throughout the suite. "Why are you being so horrible? It's not enough I have to put up with him? You used to be human. What happened?"

He froze his expression. "I wised up."

"You mean, you sold out."

"I'd sold out long before I met you," he said in that same strange whisper.

"So why did you help me? Huh? What was in it for you?"

He gave her a smile he'd perfected under Todd's tutelage, then leaned in so his lips nearly touched the perfect shell of her ear. "I got you in the sack, didn't I?"

When he leaned back, the fire had left her eyes to be replaced by nothing so much as utter defeat. He hoped… God, he hoped, the fire wasn't gone forever.

EDWARD POTEREIKO SWORE and stamped his feet to keep his circulation flowing. He glanced at the stainless-steel watch he'd gotten as a retirement gift after twenty-five years in the GRU, and saw that it was two-fifteen.

Late. His contact was late. The breakup of the Soviet Union had, in the former colonel's opinion, also broken much of the vigor and discipline of the Ukrainian army. Now they were just so many ragtag costumed clowns playing at being soldiers. In his day, Edward would have had a number of them shot. The remainder would damn well have been on time.

He peered across the frozen moonlit fields toward the lights of Kharkiv, trying to ignore the condensation of breath on his glasses. He willed himself to see a figure struggling across the tundra in the rising fog. Still nothing moved.

Cursing again, he considered sitting in his four-door Volga sedan with the engine running and the heater blasting, but decided the risk was not worth the comfort. He turned his back to the lights and stuffed a Bogatyri cigarette between his lips, his American lighter shrouded by his greatcoat.

He'd barely puffed the hot ash to incandescent redness when he heard the crunch of boots approaching. He cautiously moved to place the sedan between himself and the sound. A dark silhouette stumbled into view, visible breath rasping in the misty silence, the telltale peak of the Russian army cap obvious against the distant twinkling lights.

As the figure moved closer, Potereiko could see the

reason for the shadow's stumbling gait; the man was carrying a large metal suitcase that hit his leg with every step. "Colonel?" he whispered. "Colonel?"

Potereiko stepped from behind the sedan and puffed on his cigarette before speaking, blowing smoke in a thick cloud that drifted sinuously over his shoulder. "You're late, Vanko."

Vanko dropped the suitcase at the rear of the Volga sedan with a sharp crunch that made the other man start involuntarily, although he knew it would take more than that for the case to begin its deadly work. Vanko pulled his gloves off and blew on his bare hands to warm them. "The security guard at the factory demanded extra money, just as I was leaving. He thinks I'm stealing computers." He laughed, then sniffed at the smoke from Potereiko's cigarette. "Hey, let me have one of those."

"You were supposed to be here twenty minutes ago," Potereiko said. "I've got to be back at the border before the shift changes at three." He fished out one of the unfiltered Bogatyris and handed it to Vanko, then lit it for him.

"The guard—"

"Forget the guard." Potereiko waved his arm dismissively and opened the trunk of the Volga. As the lid opened, a light came on inside. "Let's see it."

"Ah, Colonel."

"I want to make sure it's what you say, Vanko."

"Would I try to cheat you?"

"You're already trying to get a few extra rubles for the greedy guard. Open the case." Potereiko stood back, hands in his pockets, cigarette dangling from between his lips.

Vanko flipped a pair of latches, not unlike a briefcase, and carefully raised the lid, exposing a neatly machined panel containing an array of readouts and switches, barely visible in the dim trunk light. "You can set a code to open it. Here." Vanko indicated a spot near one of the latches on the inside of the case.

Edward moved closer and peered in. "Ah, yes. I remember when we were designing these." He reached out a hand and caressed the panel, almost fondly. "We were going to destroy the Americans." He closed the case, then the trunk.

"Those were the days, eh, comrade?" Vanko said.

Potereiko puffed on his cigarette, regarded the hot ember, then dropped the butt and ground it out with the sole of his shoe. "There's much more opportunity now," he said.

"Speaking of opportunity…" Vanko puffed his own cigarette, hands in his coat pockets, gloves tucked beneath an armpit.

"Of course. The money."

"I had to give the guard an extra fifty rubles."

"Let's see," Potereiko said as he reached inside his coat. He pulled out a pistol.

Vanko's eyes widened and he backed up a step, pulling his arms from his pockets, gloves falling to the ground. "What is this?"

"This is a Smith & Wesson .38-caliber Police Special," Potereiko said calmly. "Made in America. New Jersey, I believe. Nice, is it not?"

"Edward… Colonel… Please."

"You are a symbol of all that's gone wrong with the Soviet Union, Vanko. And a petty thinker, to boot." In one smooth motion former Colonel Edward Potereiko raised the weapon and fired, striking Vanko in the forehead. As the roar of the gun died, his face, only slightly marred by the entry wound, took on a startled look. The cigarette fell from his lips, lodging on his heavy coat before he fell backward.

Potereiko put the gun back inside his coat and checked his watch. He still had fifteen minutes to get back to the border, and it was only six or seven miles. He was, in fact, far more concerned with the nearly six thousand miles he'd have to drive in the next week. He stepped over Vanko's body.

"Das vadanya, comrade."

Chapter Four

Jenny turned away, unable to look at Nick. God, had she made it all up? Had this man ever truly been kind to her?

She ran her hand over the cold relief of a standing screen, her fingers tracing the edges of a reclining jaguar as she ran through a dozen quick memories, Nick gentle in all of them. He'd been tough in front of Todd and Sweet, of course, but when they'd been alone…

She remembered the first time he'd kissed her. They'd been in her bathroom, of all places, standing by the Jacuzzi. He'd found a narrow window where Todd's hidden cameras couldn't see, and he'd led her there, positioned her just so. They'd had to whisper, although the sound of the bubbling water had masked their voices. And in that tiny space of freedom, that narrow gap between the nightmare of her life and the promise of something too good to be anything but a dream, he'd caressed her hair with trembling fingers, searched her gaze for secrets, then leaned down and touched her lips ever so softly with his own.

He'd lingered there, just brushing lips to lips, breathing his breath into her, filling her with desire. He'd been patient, maddeningly so, and finally she'd been the one to deepen the kiss, to open her lips and take a forbidden taste of this man who was her protector and her prison guard.

He'd moaned, so loudly she'd been afraid, but then the fear didn't matter. Nothing mattered but his arms around her, the hard warmth of his chest, his tongue doing wicked, wonderful things that made her forget reality.

It had only lasted a few minutes. A few precious, dangerous minutes. But in that time, she'd felt a connection that had given her the strength to do the unthinkable. She'd decided, at that moment, when she couldn't distinguish between his breath and hers, that she would escape. And that someday, when they were both free of the monster in the other room, they would meet again.

The man behind her bore no resemblance to the man in her mind's eye. They looked the same, but they were complete opposites when it came to the heart.

What had happened to him? Was being around Todd enough to kill that humanity? She closed her eyes. Of course it was. If she'd stayed, who knows what would have happened to her? What was of much more concern now was what would happen to her baby. How could he ever come out of this unscathed?

"What did he tell you?"

She turned to face Nick again, hardening herself against the cool disdain in his gaze. "I have to dress. Go back to him."

"Then, what are you waiting for?"

He was actually more beautiful when he was like

this. When his lip had that hint of a sneer and his eyes burned right through her. But she knew better than anyone that beauty was nothing. A trap. A web.

Without giving him the satisfaction of an answer, she headed for the bedroom. Todd wanted her hair down. She'd have to wear full makeup, which she hadn't done since the day she'd left him. And wear the awful lingerie that was sure to be in her dresser.

The bedroom, as large as her living room and kitchen combined, had been redecorated in the same motif as the rest of the suite. The four-poster was swathed in sheer white drapes, the posts themselves sturdy brass. Looking at the bed made her stomach clench as other memories came back, piling in her head like a car wreck.

When they'd first met, Todd had been a perfect gentleman. He'd courted her with respect, giving her all the time she'd needed to make her decisions. Even after they'd made love, he was patient, showing her a side of him she knew now to be a complete charade.

Only when she was well and truly trapped did he come out, show her his true colors. Sick colors. His cruelty became masterful in the bedroom. What he'd done to her, made her do...

She took a deep breath as she thrust the thoughts from her consciousness. Striding to the closet, she flung open the doors, determined to think of nothing but the task at hand.

The wardrobe was far sparser than she'd imagined. Half a dozen dresses, another half dozen negligees. High heels, of course, and gaudy accessories. Furs, jeweled handbags. Not her taste, not her style. They made her feel cheap, despite their astronomical price tags.

She picked out the skimpiest dress. The night was going to be horrible. Painful. She'd do well to mitigate her circumstances wherever she could, beginning with the slit-up-to-there gold lamé dress that hardly covered her breasts and bared her back completely. There would be no bra, not with this dress, and no hose. In the top dresser drawer she found several pairs of the tiniest thongs she'd ever seen, mere teasing of fabric. She put on the white ones.

As she dressed, she turned it all off. Her repulsion, her fear, her worry for Patrick. She turned it off and went as far deep inside as she could. It had been a long time since she'd taken refuge there, but she found her safe zone waiting, as if she'd never left.

She took her hair down as she walked to the bathroom, there to painstakingly put on the makeup of a showgirl. No. Of a whore. By the time she was finished, with only five minutes to spare, she hardly recognized herself.

Which, she supposed, was a good thing.

She checked her reflection, made sure he'd approve, then grabbed a gold handbag and slipped on the four-inch heels that hurt with her first step. It didn't matter. That would be the least of her discomfort tonight.

NICK HAD MADE a few phone calls while Jenny was dressing, one of them real. Jed Tyler, his mechanic, told him his Porsche was ready, after having the brakes re-

lined. During the call, and the other two, one to find out
the correct time, and the other to a number he knew had
been disconnected, he walked around the living room
as if studying the decor. His real quest was to find the
hidden cameras. As he'd suspected, they had all been
moved during the redecoration. It had taken him a long
time to find the six cameras before, and so far he'd only
identified three.

He'd ferret out the bugs later. He'd be spending a lot
of time here while he made Jenny uncomfortable
enough to insist he be replaced. Which needed to be
damn soon. He had to be free to find out what the hell
Todd was planning. It was big. Bigger than anything
he'd encountered so far and it had nothing to do with
the casino.

Todd was one of the wealthiest men in Nevada—in
the world. And still he wasn't satisfied. What he wanted
to be when he grew up was an arms dealer. Like Adnan
Khashoggi at his peak, only richer. He wanted to sell big
toys like F/A-18 Hornet jets and Black Hawk attack hel-
icopters, but the U.S. government had restricted his ability to play in the billion-dollar playgrounds. Oh, he
could sell arms, but he'd have to get out of the casino
business.

Todd continued to host the world's largest arms trade
shows, however, with representatives from all corners
of the globe. He was the world's leading exporter of sig-
nals intelligence. The interception, exploitation and
jamming of electronic communication; a multibillion-
dollar enterprise designed to eavesdrop on the conver-

sations and data traffic of U.S. adversaries anywhere on earth. Real James Bond stuff.

The arms shows were more exciting to him than any poker tournament could hope to be. His contacts were world-class, although the meetings were never in Nevada. Rio, South Africa, Kashmir; Todd jetted all over the globe in his pursuit of the highest bidder for his wares. His presence at defense conferences were high-ticket events, where he would dine with presidents and kings, many of whom where high on the U.S. government's list of unfriendlies.

Nick had gone to several arms shows with the boss and had seen his share of what went on in the world of covert ops. Gambling, even at the level played at Xanadu, couldn't hold a candle to the stakes that were played on that field.

What Nick had also seen was that Todd was not a man to give up easily. His goal was for the big score, the billions that would make him untouchable. Since the powers that be had told him he couldn't sell weapons, Nick knew that was exactly what Todd would do. Not conventional weapons. He'd take that extra step, that mass-destruction step that would tell the world exactly who they were messing with. C. Randall Todd was going nuclear. Nick knew it, he just couldn't prove it. Not yet.

What Nick did know was that Todd had found a supplier, an ex-military from the defunct Soviet Union, and he had two buyers in the wings. Both of whom were enemies of the state, both of whom would have no compunction about using the nuke on American soil. The bidding continued as Todd maneuvered his players. The deal was coming to a close, time was running out.

And what Todd didn't know, what Jenny didn't know, what Nick's own mother didn't know, was that he was the man responsible for stopping it. So to say baby-sitting Jenny was *inconvenient* was something of an understatement.

He heard a footstep, turned from the Persian tapestry above the fireplace. Jenny walked in from the bedroom, totally transformed from the woman who'd cradled her son.

She looked like what Todd wanted her to be: the world's most expensive mistress. The gown looked painted on, what there was of it. The neckline was so low, he was afraid for her to move, and yet when she did walk, nothing showed but what she intended. Her face—God, that beautiful face—was so made up she was almost unrecognizable behind it. Her lashes were so thick he wondered how she could keep her eyes open, and her scarlet lips were as deep and wet as fresh blood.

"You look—"

"Like a whore?"

"Cold."

She shifted her gaze to his, but she'd shut herself down, made herself unreadable. "Right. Cold."

"Where's he taking you?"

She turned her gaze to her handbag. "I have no idea."

"Wasn't there something else in there? Something a little more discreet?"

"Yes. But I'm better off in this."

"Why?" he whispered, ever mindful of hidden microphones. "So you can show off to all his cronies?"

She pushed her hair behind her ear as she turned to skim his cheek with her warm breath. "What do you care? We all know what Todd likes, and what he likes is what I'm here for."

"What he likes?"

She stepped back. "Come on, Nick. Surely you can't have forgotten all of Todd's little games. It hasn't been that long."

"Yeah, I remember."

"Right. Now, if you'll excuse me, I can't afford to be late."

He was once again hit by the scent that had haunted his dreams. Her scent. "Let's go," he said as he opened the door.

She hesitated, but only for a moment. Then she lifted her shoulders, straightened her back and headed down the hall.

It felt as though he was taking her down the Green Mile, right to the executioner's block. He didn't know details about Todd's private life, but he'd heard rumors. The one thing Nick did know was that Todd wanted complete obedience from his women. How he got it was what troubled Nick.

It didn't matter. It wasn't his business. He only wished he could offer her hope, or even comfort. At the very least he wanted to tell her he was more than he seemed, that he wasn't a bastard. But that could end up very badly. For lots and lots of people. So he kept his expression neutral, his body several steps behind her, his gaze just over her left shoulder.

All he could do was look forward to the end, to the day he put Todd down once and for all. Todd was going to pay for a multitude of sins, and Nick would take great pleasure teaching him the error of his ways.

Until then, he couldn't afford to be distracted, not even by Jenny.

UP UNTIL THE last second, the very moment before the door to Todd's suite opened, she hoped Nick would stop it. That he'd reach over, touch her, save her.

By the time it was too late, she'd gotten it. Gotten the truth about Nick. The reality of her situation. She was on her own. No one was going to help, no one was going to care. She had to get Patrick out. And she had to do it alone.

But first she had to get through the night.

"Ah, that's my girl." Todd stepped into the foyer, dressed in an Armani tux, his silver-white hair shining in the lights of his chandelier. "That's the beauty I fell in love with."

She forced a smile. "You look very handsome."

He came close, his scent assaulting her, making it hard to keep her smile steady. "Thank you, my love." He stood in front of her, lifted her chin with the back of his hand until their eyes met. She gasped when she saw the malice in his gaze. He was enjoying every second of this, her knowing he was going to hurt her. Hurt her badly.

He leaned down, touched her lips with his.

She let him kiss her, forced herself to kiss him back. The moment she increased the pressure, he pulled back, keeping the contact light, almost tender. And then he nipped her.

She gasped, stepped back.

Todd laughed. Turned away. "Nick, my man. Go on, get the hell out of here. Find that pretty dancer you like so much." He reached into his pocket, pulled out a wad of bills, tossed them to Nick. "Take her somewhere nice. I won't need you till tomorrow."

Nick grinned, put the money in his pocket. "Thank you, sir. I'll be here first thing."

"Make it about nine. I have a feeling we'll be sleeping in."

"You got it. I'll have the cell with me if you need me tonight."

But Todd wasn't listening. He'd turned his attention back to Jenny, dismissing Nick as effectively as if he'd shown him the door.

Jenny watched Nick out of the corner of her eye. He never looked back. The door closed with a click and Todd's hand landed on her shoulder. He squeezed her there, squeezed hard enough to make her moan.

"You know where I want you," he said, his voice low, soft, almost purring.

She swallowed. "Yes, sir." Then she turned, headed toward the bedroom. She kept her head high, willed herself to stop trembling. But each step was more difficult than the last.

NICK WENT RIGHT to his room, to his bathroom, and started the shower. When he'd locked the door, he stripped, but before he got under the water, he pulled a small black pouch from under the sink. It looked like an iPod. He put the earphones on, pressed Play. But instead of the sounds of music, he heard a guttural laugh. Todd's laugh.

The bug was in Todd's living room. It was an extraordinary piece of equipment, built specifically to get by the sweeps of one of the world's most efficient and sophisticated counter-surveillance experts. It, and three others, were the only microphones like it in the world.

Nick listened for all he was worth. He hoped they wouldn't go to the bedroom. There were no bugs there. He'd put one inside Todd's limo. The other was in Todd's outer office. Nick had one more, but that bug hadn't been successfully planted. It was to have been in Todd's private office. The inner sanctum. But every time Nick had tried to put it there, something had stopped him. Something in the form of Henry Sweet.

He didn't care at the moment. Not when he had to listen to Todd's footsteps. Todd's laughter.

Damn. Was that whimpering? Crying? Damn it, whatever he'd heard was gone. Todd had taken her out of range.

Nick couldn't do a thing. Not at this stage of the game. But when it was over, the bastard would pay. Nick would kill him with his own two hands if he so much as raised a hand to Jenny.

Chapter Five

Jenny shifted on her seat, trying to find a position that didn't hurt, but that wasn't possible, even on the over-stuffed chairs at Samarkand, Xanadu's most exclusive restaurant, where Todd had taken her on their first date.

The waitresses, none of whom she recognized, still wore what they used to call Jeannie costumes: gold-brocade bras, white-silk harem pants, pointy-toed shoes. None of the women were more than a size six, and they were all stunning. The competition to work here was fierce because unlike most of the gourmet restaurants on the Strip, this place hired primarily women and the tips were astronomical. Only the cocktail waitresses in the high-roller suites made more.

Jenny had been right to wear her own horrifying out-fit. The admiring glances from the mostly older men in the room gratified Todd, which mitigated his temper. Still, she felt naked, vulnerable in a way that would have brought tears to her eyes if she let it. But she had to be strong. For Patrick.

As the evening progressed and she adjusted to the

truth of her captivity, she realized that what hurt the most was Nick's complete turnabout. It just didn't make sense. She couldn't have been that wrong.

Somehow she had to get him somewhere they could talk. Somewhere outside of Todd's reach. It wouldn't be easy. God, it had taken so long for them to find all the cameras and microphones! And even when Nick was sure they'd found them all, it was still such a huge risk. To both of them.

"You don't like the veal?"

She started, shifting her attention back to Todd. She knew better than to let her thoughts wander when she was with him. He always caught her, tried to trip her up, make her show her inattention. The least bit of day-dreaming could end in another "session" with Todd showing her what focus was all about. "No, it's very good." She illustrated by taking a healthy bite, then washing it down with a sip of wine.

Had she been a guest here she would have enjoyed the meal. The food was exquisitely prepared by one of the best chefs on the planet, seduced here by Todd from his five-star restaurant in Paris. The wine list was unequaled anywhere in the U.S., and had been rated the number one cellar by both *Food and Wine* and *Wine Spectator.*

She might as well have been eating cereal. Another bite, another sip, a smile. Watch him, search for signs of a mood shift, a surprise attack; anticipate his moves, his needs. He wasn't like other people, but he knew how to pretend. Most of his employees worshipped him, although they knew better than to get on his wrong side. They compared him to a mob boss, his regime a lot like the good old days of Vegas when the police knew their place and no one got out of hand twice. If you were in his good graces, it meant immediate rewards, monetary and otherwise. Promotions, bonuses, perks. But screw up and you were not only out of work at the Xanadu, but at every other hotel on the Strip.

She'd never liked Las Vegas. She'd only come here because U.N.L.V. was the only school that had offered her a scholarship. They paid for tuition, but Jenny had had to work to earn the rest, and where better to earn quick bucks than at a casino? She'd gotten a job as a cocktail waitress the day she'd turned twenty-one.

It had been a real learning experience for a girl from Kenosha, Wisconsin, but she'd been friendly and the tips had been more than she'd ever dreamed of earning from a part-time job. She'd even managed to buy herself a little used car, get herself some decent clothes and have a few bucks left over to take in some of the shows from time to time, when she wasn't studying. Her life had been good and her prospects bright.

Then she'd met Todd and she'd gone right through the looking glass.

He'd dazzled her from the first. That he'd even noticed her had floored her. Soon, she was going to the finest restaurants, meeting celebrities, being picked up in limos and riding in private jets. He'd been the perfect gentleman, never pressing her, never trying to take things too fast.

She'd held off sleeping with him for a long time. Almost five months. But he'd made her feel ungrateful and selfish, and she'd given in and, even then, although she wasn't sure she loved him, he'd been gentle, kind, patient.

He'd begged her to give up the job, to move into her own suite at the hotel, always assuring her that he only wanted what was best for her. Like a fool, she'd let diamonds get into her eyes, and it wasn't long until she'd given up her dreams of a business degree, and she was his.

The last remnant of her old life left with the sale of her little Mazda, and that's when things started to get weird. Nick had been her friend, her confidant. Todd had explained that she was vulnerable because of what she meant to him, that she needed protection, and she'd gone along with it, never realizing until too late that while Nick prevented anyone from getting to her, he also prevented her from getting out.

It all became real clear the day she watched Todd order someone's execution. Oh, yeah. The picture had come into razor-sharp focus. Along with the knowledge there was no way out.

"I would think after all this time away, you would be brimming with questions," Todd said.

She nodded. "I don't know where to begin."

He laughed. Anyone walking by would have thought they were having a wonderful time. "Let me guide you, dear Jenny. As in all things."

It wasn't sarcasm or wit. "Thank you."

He signaled the waitress for another drink. He always

had the same thing. Single malt scotch, aged a minimum of twenty-five years, straight up. "I'm a much wealthier man, for starters," he said. "Plenty for Patrick to inherit." He paused, narrowed his pale blue eyes. "A son, Jenny. You knew how important that is to me."

"Of course, Todd. I'm sorry. I wasn't thinking."

"No. You were thinking. Only of yourself, however. Not of Patrick's welfare. Did you honestly believe any child of mine should be raised in a place like Milford, Utah? That he should go to public schools? Jenny," he said, shaking his head, "haven't I taught you anything? Even if you were willing to slum it, he's not your private property."

"That's true. I know you can give him everything, that you can make his future wonderful."

"That nanny used to work for Princess Diana. She knows how to train a child to accept special privileges and responsibilities. You coddle the boy, and that's going to stop. He's not too young to learn his place in the world. Does he read?"

"Not yet, Todd. He's not even three."

"I read when I was three."

She smiled, batted her heavy eyelashes. "You're the exception to every rule."

"As my son will be."

"I'll start working on it tomorrow."

"The nanny will see to that. Tomorrow, you're going shopping. I want you to have your wardrobe complete by the end of the week. Don't get any jewelry. I'll see to that."

The waitress came by with his drink, and then she refreshed Jenny's water. Jenny made sure not to look at her. When they were alone again, Todd sipped his Scotch, reached into his jacket pocket and pulled out one of his Cuban cigars. She hated them. They smelled bad and made his breath terrible.

"I'm going to be hosting a very large party on the Fourth of July. I'm getting rid of the El Rio, imploding the damn thing. I suppose you heard I got the approval for the new hotel."

"It was all over the news."

"The government tried to hold up the plans. I swear, the country is going right down the toilet."

She turned her head slightly to the side as she slowly finished her meal, listening to his diatribe on how stupid everyone was in the government, how he was smarter than all of them, which would have been amusing if it wasn't probably true. She'd heard it all before, over and over and over.

Still, she couldn't tune him out. She didn't dare. Something might have changed and she'd better be able to spot it if it had.

It was as if the world had stopped here. The past two and a half years were like some kind of dream. His ego, his temper, none of it had changed since the last time she'd seen him. Even the way he puffed his stupid cigar, as if no one else deserved any air, hadn't altered a bit.

But she'd changed. She was older, wiser and, most important, she was a mother. Nothing mattered to her except Patrick. She would get him out of here, get him free. She had no idea how, but she'd figure it out. She'd done it once, she could do it again.

Last time, she'd had help. If there was a God, she'd have help again. She just had to get to Nick. Find out what had changed him. And how to change him back.

She needed him. In more ways than one.

NICK SAT UP in bed, gasping. Jenny. Her cries had pierced him as sharply as any knife and he had to do something. *Now.*

His bedroom came into focus, the framed print of a khalakha saddle across from his bed, right next to his mounted TV monitor; his dresser and the mirror above it; his own reflection, sweaty, hair all over the place, pasty beneath his tan.

Damn it. It was a dream. A stupid dream.

Nick ran a hand over his face, rubbed the sleep out of his eyes, then climbed out of bed. He wasn't looking forward to the day. Now, more than ever, he didn't want to do what he had to. Jenny needed...

Screw that. Save Jenny or stop a madman from killing who knows how many? He had no choice. It would all work out in the end. But only if he did his job.

Only if he got the hell away from Jenny and her problems.

The timing on this couldn't have been worse. He had to let Owen know that his situation had changed. That meant he had to be free of Jenny and Todd's surveillance long enough to make a phone call. He'd work that out.

It was just past five-thirty. He slipped on running

shorts and his footgear, and after he finished his crunches, headed out for his run. He didn't take his phone. There was too great a chance he'd run into Sweet.

SHE SHOWERED until the skin on her fingertips pruned, and still she couldn't get the feel of him off her. Her hopes that he'd leave her be at the end of the night had been foolish, she realized now. She should have prepared herself. Wishing for things that couldn't be was wasteful, and she wouldn't do it again. It made her weak and she needed to be strong.

She didn't, wouldn't, categorize her escape as wishful thinking. But to make it a reality, she had to be as focused as a laser. That meant total acceptance of what was in order to create that which would be.

While she was here, she belonged to Todd. She was his toy, his lapdog, and being an obedient lapdog was the only way to minimize punishment. It was also useless to dream she could be good enough to escape any punishment, because he didn't need an excuse. Excuses were merely conveniences.

So she'd be good. Attentive. She'd even pretend not to be repulsed. Which wouldn't be as hard as it could have been. He'd never focused his energy sexually. He preferred dominance. Power trips. There was little doubt in her mind that when he masturbated, if he masturbated, it was to thoughts of Steve Wynn losing money, not her in a string bikini.

All that worked in her favor. Once he felt certain of her obedience, he'd leave her alone for the most part.

She'd be expected to appear at his side whenever necessary, boost his ego when alone, and from time to time he'd treat her cruelly. She could take it.

What she didn't know was how much control he was going to give the nanny. Todd wasn't going to let Jenny have free rein with Patrick, of course. But if she could show that Patrick would learn better, behave better, in her presence, then she might be able to have access to him.

If Todd decided to take Patrick away, everything was lost. She had to move fast, move carefully, and have a plan. Right now, that meant finding a way to talk to Nick. She had to go shopping, and she assumed Nick would be her watchdog. She just hoped Todd was sure enough about Nick to send him alone.

Once in the stores, she could find a moment, although she had to be careful, even then. Todd was full of surprises and having spies in the stores wouldn't shock her in the least.

Discretion. A level head. Focus. The goal was to survive, to escape. And this time, to get so far away Todd would never find her.

Jenny turned off the water. She stepped out into his bathroom and took one of the heated towels from the rack. She wrapped herself in the finest Egyptian cotton, dried off. Put on the white-silk robe, dried her hair, brushing it carefully, and once it was the way Todd liked it, she patiently applied her makeup. Not as heavily as last night, but more than she would ever choose for herself. Only after she'd put on the last coat of lip gloss did she leave the bathroom.

He was up, of course, standing by his floor-to-ceiling window, surveying the town he called his domain. He was on the phone.

The butler had brought in coffee and the morning rolls Todd liked. She sat at her place, smiling as Todd looked her way. He dismissed her without acknowledgment, so she went on to eat, to drink her coffee and wait. He'd let her know when she could leave.

She studied the room, learning details, making mental notes, but his conversation caught her attention. He was speaking to someone who didn't have a clear line, as his shouting was more about being heard than cowing the listener.

"I told you, Potereiko, I need you here by July fourth. Not a day later. If you screw me on this, my friend…"

Something about that name rang a bell.

"Our Middle Eastern associate will be here in two weeks. He knows his bid was preempted. He'll come up with something substantially larger, I assure you."

She'd met a man named Potereiko once. He was from Russia, or Yugoslavia, or someplace like that. A big man, with bad teeth and the breath to go with them. He'd been an intermediary back then, for some equipment Todd was selling. They hadn't met in Vegas. It was in Rio, at Defentech, the arms show, back in 1999. That's right. They'd had dinner and the entertainment after had been a sex show. Potereiko had been terribly uncomfortable.

He'd struck her as the kind of man who'd always followed orders. That the dissolution of the Soviet Union had broken something in him, too. In fact, she'd rather liked him. Until, and she remembered this quite clearly, she'd looked into his eyes. The coldness there had made her think of Siberia. Of death.

"Just get it here on time, Edward."

She went back to her coffee, not wanting to give Todd any reason to think she'd been listening, even though she'd have to have been deaf not to. He hung up the phone, came over to her, lifted her chin. "You look lovely."

She smiled a puppet's grin. Forced her eyes to admire, her voice to please. This was her life now. This never-ending nightmare.

JENNY KNOCKED on the door, desperate to see Patrick, to know if he was okay. She couldn't stand the separation, it was like taking away the most important part of her, and she could put up with almost anything, including Todd, as long as she could be with her baby.

The door to the nanny's suite opened slowly and Mrs. Norris, dressed in a dark blue shirtdress, smiled a welcome. "I know a little boy who's going to be very happy."

"Where is he?"

The answer came from Patrick. He'd caught sight of his mommy and screamed with such intensity Jenny thought her heart would break. So overwhelmed at seeing her, he couldn't even walk, Patrick sat in the middle of the Persian carpet, held his arms outstretched and howled.

Jenny ran to him, scooped him up and kissed him

over and over, petting him, smelling him, her own tears mixing with his on both their cheeks.

She rocked him back and forth, barely aware of Mrs. Norris who was making her way to the bedroom, and Jenny whispered her thanks for a nanny so human and understanding. Something she had no reason to expect in this horrible place.

"Honey, shh," she said, petting his hair. "It's okay. Mommy's right here."

He couldn't speak yet, although his sobs weren't quite as loud and he was breathing again.

"I'll never leave you, sweetheart. Never. I'm just next door, just like in the old house, when I had my room and you had yours."

"Mommy…"

"I know, baby. I know."

She closed her eyes, hefted him higher on her chest and walked toward the door.

"Ms. Granger?"

She stopped, turned to see Mrs. Norris standing by a car that she'd seen priced in an FAO Schwartz toy catalog for almost a thousand dollars. "Yes?"

"I'm sorry, miss. But Mr. Todd was most explicit in his instructions."

"What instructions?"

The older woman blushed as she approached, folded her hands across her stomach as if she was going to pray. "He told me quite firmly that Patrick wasn't to leave here without his permission."

"I'm just taking him to my room. It's next door."

"I understand, and I'm terribly sorry. But he specified this circumstance exactly. And I'm afraid I can't let you take the boy."

"Come with me, then. I can't leave him. He's just a baby. He doesn't understand."

"I'm sorry, dear. Truly. But perhaps if I called Mr. Todd…"

"And say what? That I want to be with my own child? Why should he have anything to say about this? Patrick is my baby."

"I know. And I'm not at all sure what the situation is between you and Mr. Todd, but, dear, I know one thing." She came to stand next to Jenny and put a hand on her shoulder. "I'm willing to bend over backward to see that you and Patrick have as much time with each other as possible. I don't care if you're here twenty-four hours a day." She leaned in, lowered her voice. "But I've also worked for men like Mr. Todd before and I know that he'll dismiss me in a heartbeat if I disobey such an order so quickly. And then, who knows who will take my place? So why don't we see how things play out over time, yes? For now, let's be good soldiers. We'll make accommodations as soon as it's possible."

Jenny stared at the woman, surprised at the level of understanding, and her logic. Of course she didn't want to part with Patrick, but, as in all things to do with Todd, patience would win out over obstinacy.

As much as it killed her, she'd play along. For now. "I have to go shopping, but as soon as I come back, I'll come see you, my sweet boy."

He gripped her tighter, digging his little fingernails into her arms.

"I know, it's hard, baby, but it's just for a bit. Just like going to see Alice when Mommy went to work, remember? I came and got you every single day, isn't that right?"

Patrick's face squeezed into a grimace, the prelude to another round of sobs.

"You have to be brave, Patrick. Be brave for Mommy, okay?"

Mrs. Norris held out her arms and Jenny gathered every ounce of courage she had to hand her boy over. She couldn't hold her own tears back. "I'll be back soon, honey. I promise."

Mrs. Norris peeled him away, held him close, gave Jenny a sympathetic smile.

Coward that she was, Jenny had to get away. His cries tore her apart, ripped her very soul out. She ran to the door. Into the arms of Nick Mason.

She didn't mean to crumble, but her legs wouldn't hold her. Nick held her, held her close. And she heard, as if from far away, his voice, no more than a whisper.

"The bastard is going to pay."

Chapter Six

Nick held her as she wept, the child's cry still echoing in the hallway. He shouldn't hold her like this, it was exactly the kind of situation where he should be a bastard, but he couldn't do that to Jenny. God only knew what Todd had put her through last night. He didn't see any marks on her. At least there was that.

All he wanted to do was to comfort her. To take her as far away from the hotel as he could. What the hell kind of a man was he that he couldn't harden his heart when he knew what was at stake? When Todd pulled off his plan, when he had a weapon that could destroy half the country, would Nick comfort himself with the thought that he'd been a pal? A regular sweetheart?

He took hold of her arms and pulled her to her feet, held back his urge to shake her. "We have to go," he said harshly, making sure she knew he meant business.

It worked. She stopped crying. With red-rimmed eyes, she stared at him, the hurt, the confusion, as painful as a blow. "What the hell happened to you?" she whispered.

"I don't know what you mean."

"You know who he is. Is that what you want? To be like him? To be so hateful that I can't stand for you to look at me?"

"That would be a start," he said.

Her eyes closed and she stepped back, wrenching herself free. "Fine. So be it. You can go to hell at his side."

"I've already got my ticket," he said. "In the meantime, I've got the credit card and the limo. You need to get dressed so we can go."

She turned her back, wiped her eyes with the backs of her hands. Her makeup smeared and somehow the dark smudges brought back in brutal detail the morning after the first night they'd spent together. She'd been so delicate in his arms, he'd been terrified of bruising her. She'd had dark smudges under her eyes then, but they hadn't been makeup. Stress had put the darkness there. Fear. The marks she tried so hard to cover up with all that damned makeup.

"I'll be ten minutes," she said. "I don't suppose you want to meet me at the car."

"I have my orders."

"Yeah. Orders." She walked away, the spirit that he'd seen in her carriage last night gone, locked behind the door of the nanny's room along with her son.

He followed her, aware of the cameras hidden in the walls, the ears that were always listening, the eyes that never blinked. He couldn't be so much of an ass that Todd would fire him. It was a fine line. One he had to find, and toe.

She kept her distance as he unlocked her door, then she swept past him. He let her go, feigned a casual air as he went inside.

He'd worn pressed slacks, a pale blue polo shirt and a light sport coat for their trip to the Forum Shops. He needed to look sharp, but not like a maître d'. One thing he'd learned from working for Todd was how to dress. He could have lived without the lesson.

He didn't sit. Instead, as Jenny dressed, he cruised the living room. In his breast pocket he had a bug finder, an Omni Spectral Correlator, that would not only detect any kind of monitoring equipment, whether operating or not, but also record the exact location in the walls via a highly sensitized GPS, so that when he came back in the following days, he would be able to draw vectors of fields of vision, map the room according to the sweep of a lens.

As for the microphones, those could be neutralized, at least temporarily, once he understood the type and frequency of the equipment. It was difficult because Todd used the most sophisticated gear on the planet, which his companies, here and abroad, designed and manufactured. On the plus side, Nick had unique access to state-of-the-art implements and could be reasonably certain that his efforts would be effective.

Reasonably certain wasn't good enough, but it would have to do. Regardless of his findings and his counter-measures, he would continue to be careful. Any misstep could be more costly than he dared to imagine.

Jenny came back into the room and he was amazed

at her ability to get it together. No one would have a clue what she'd just been through this morning or last night. She wore a sleeveless pink dress that came down to midthigh, high-heeled sandals, gold hoops in her ears. Her hair cascaded in soft waves across her shoulders. He wished like hell she didn't have to put all that crap on her face, but damn it, she was a beauty. She looked like summer.

"Let's go," she said.

He nodded; went to the door. "After you."

She walked by him, the metal back in her spine. She was the kind of woman he'd want on his team. Who would come through no matter what the odds. He hoped she would come through this. She deserved so much more.

They walked silently, her matching him stride for stride. She didn't even glance at her son's room when they passed it. As they approached the elevator, he caught sight of their image in the mirror. They looked like a model couple on vacation, perhaps even on their honeymoon. She so blond and slender, him in his crisp slacks and his Bruno Magli shoes and his Prada sport coat. Like one of the commercials for Xanadu.

It made sense that Todd would bring her back now, right when it was all coming to a head. He needed to show her what a big man he was. It wasn't enough that he had more millions than he'd ever be able to spend. That he donated more to charity than the net worth of several Third World countries. Not that Todd gave a damn about anyone, but it looked good, and Todd needed to look good.

Jenny did that for him. Made him look good. He could have had anyone, and in the past couple of years he'd gone through gorgeous women like used tissues. From movie stars to models to showgirls, Todd had them all. None of them was Jenny.

She had something so… He'd figured it out, actually. It was a certain kind of charisma, a combination of beauty, grace, strength and magic. Yeah, magic.

And the bastard wanted to crush that out of her. Smart. Real smart.

The elevator door opened, but the ride down was silent, uncomfortable. Jenny stared straight ahead, never looking at him, not once.

Kahrim, Todd's driver, was waiting outside when they got down to the lobby. He nodded at Nick, walked around to open the door for Jenny.

Kahrim hadn't been around when Jenny was here before. He'd been hired shortly after she'd left. He was a hell of a well-trained bodyguard, and as far as Nick's information went, he was legit. No underworld ties, no foreign complications. Just a guy who could drive his way out of any situation, shoot like a marksman and generally mess up anyone this side of a tank. A good man to have as a friend.

"How you doin', Kahrim?"

"Good, Mr. Nick. Better than yesterday, that's for sure."

"This is Jenny. She's a special friend of Mr. Todd's."

"I know, Mr. Nick." He helped Jenny into the back seat, then leaned over, blocking her from the street. "You need anything, Miss Jenny, you just let me know."

"Thank you."

Nick got in on the other side and leaned back for the short ride down the Strip to Caesar's. All he had to do was to wait a few more minutes. They'd be at the Forum Shops. They'd be alone. Of course, he had no idea what in hell he was going to say to her. He couldn't tell her the truth.

As strong as Jenny was, she couldn't help her own natural reactions. If she knew who he really was, she might give something away. It would be inadvertent, but that wouldn't matter. The consequences would be the same as if she ratted him out.

He had to keep her in the dark.

When it was over, he was gonna give this crap up. No more hiding. No more subterfuge. Maybe he'd run away to the mountains. Or the ocean. Not the desert.

He glanced at Jenny, who sat as still as a stone as they made their slow way down the Strip. It didn't seem to matter what time of year, or time of day, Las Vegas Boulevard was always too crowded, too full of tourists.

Nick could see Kahrim's curious glances in the rear-view mirror, but he ignored them. It wasn't so easy to ignore Jenny. Tension came off her in waves, sitting in her silence. His hand was so close to hers. If he could just…

He turned, looked out the shaded window, stared blankly as monuments to excess slipped past.

When they got to Caesar's Palace, Kahrim let Jenny out. Nick told him he'd call for a pickup in a few hours. The older man seemed hesitant, but Nick assured him it was all right. Todd had given him clear instructions. They'd meet at the same place.

Jenny walked ahead of him, knowing her way through the high-end mall. She barely looked at the Roman statues, the columns, the fantastical art that made the Forum Shops such a tourist trap. Even the huge fish tank near the Cheesecake Factory didn't warrant a glance, and that had been one of Jenny's favorites in the past.

They headed first to Armani. After that, she'd go to Versace, Max Mara, Fendi, Bebe, Prada, Ferragamo, DKNY and finally Victoria's Secret. He fully expected to spend at least a hundred thousand dollars. Jenny wouldn't like any of the clothes, he was sure of that, too. She'd especially hate shopping at Victoria's Secret.

He leaned against the wall at Armani, watching her go through clothes that made no sense to him. The well-dressed salesclerk hovered, anxious to be of assistance. She'd wet herself when she found out who was paying for this jaunt.

JENNY LOOKED at each garment with an exacting eye. Todd had very meticulous taste and she had come to know and loathe it. He wanted to flaunt her, to show her off like a racehorse wearing his colors. He also wanted even the most casual observer to know without doubt that her clothes cost a fortune.

She handed the salesgirl a half-dozen garments, then followed her to a dressing room that was decorated more extravagantly than her home in Milford. Despite the night she'd spent, the reality of the situation all around her, she could barely believe she was buying these clothes to be the best-dressed prisoner in history. In a sane world, she'd be able to turn the bastard in and lock him up for years.

Never happen. There wasn't a cop in town she could truly trust. Not that there weren't honest cops. She just had no way of knowing which ones were strong enough to resist Todd's machine. And she had no idea how far up the law-enforcement ladder his power went.

Her gaze went to the door as she pulled a cream silk shift over her head. Nick was just outside, lounging against the wall. Why him? Why couldn't her jailer have been someone else?

Being around him was too much. She had the strength to bear Todd, the strength to put up with his cruelty, but she wasn't strong enough to stand so close to Nick Mason and know that he felt nothing. Worse than nothing.

He was Patrick's father. So much of the reason she loved Patrick so much. He was like Nick. That used to be a comfort, but now it terrified her. Neither Nick nor Todd could know the truth about Patrick. Todd would kill her, probably Patrick. And if Nick found out…

Would he help her then? Would he turn back into the old Nick? Or would a child put too much of a crimp in his plans? She had no idea if she could trust him. And if there was any chance that his knowing could hurt Patrick, she'd take the secret to her grave.

She just had to be careful not to let Todd see Patrick and Nick together. She'd have to be careful around Mrs. Norris, too. She'd see that Patrick's grin was just like his daddy's.

If she could just understand who Nick was. What confused her was his whisper when she'd collapsed in his arms. He'd sounded as if he hated Todd, as if he really did want to kill him.

Yet that didn't mean his feelings had anything to do with her. He'd been hateful toward her. Cold as ice.

She looked in the mirror. The dress was too short, showed too much cleavage. Todd would approve. The next dress looked to be even worse. She'd never be able to cross her legs or bend over at all. Which meant that Todd would have her doing both things at the most embarrassing times. She had to remember it was about power, about control. She didn't have to submit even when she obeyed.

The man was sick. Seriously sick. And she had to do something before he infected her son.

Whatever it took, she was going to have to find a way out. She'd tried running away. Now she'd try something different. Sending him away.

She would send him to prison. Not for hurting her. No one on earth cared about that. But she knew secrets. She had access. And Todd, for all his posturing, was a very bad man. The illegal kind.

She would build a case strong enough to send him away for life. With the proper evidence, the state would put her and Patrick in the Witness Security Program.

It was her only hope.

She lifted the dress up, over her head. And when she could see again, Nick stood in front of her, inches away. He took the dress and tossed it to the floor.

"Listen to me," he said, his voice soft, his body tense as a bow string in the confined space. "I can't help you. I can't get you out. I can't even talk to you. Get it?"

She nodded, but she didn't think he saw her, although he was so close his breath fanned across her lips.

His hands gripped her arms. "Why the hell didn't you hide? You were out. You were free. You should have stayed away."

Jenny tried to break free, but his fingers were too tight. "You think I wanted to come back? He kidnapped Patrick. What was I supposed to do?"

Nick, red with anger, shaking, raked her face with his gaze. He looked wild, mad, and she felt something completely unexpected: fear. In all the time she'd been with Todd, she'd never been afraid of Nick, but now she struggled until he let her go, then she used her hands to cover her naked breasts. "Get out of here," she said.

"No. Not yet."

"Then give me something to wear."

He looked down. His eyebrows rose as if he'd just noticed her state of undress. "Oh, God."

She shivered at the immediate hunger in his eyes. The last time he'd seen her naked, they hadn't been able to keep themselves apart. They'd made love over and over, enduring the torture of having to be so quiet. She'd buried her face in her pillow to mute her screams of pleasure. No one had touched her the way Nick had, and she'd never felt anything like the tide of emotions that swelled when they were close.

Being with Nick had made her situation with Todd

agony. She'd never been thrilled with Todd, but once she discovered what making love should feel like, Todd's touch had repulsed her to the point of pain.

All through the past two years she'd survived on the memories of her nights with Nick. There had been so few, but she could recall everything; the slightest detail. She'd played those time and again, her only sexual release had been to sweet thoughts of his touch.

But the man who stood so close, staring at her body as if he'd never seen her before, was a stranger. She didn't understand how he could speak to her as he did, what he expected from her.

Nick closed his eyes, took a step back. He exhaled slowly and when he opened his eyes again it was to look for her dress. He reached for one of the outfits on the hook, handed it to her without meeting her gaze. "I'm sorry."

"Sorry? That's it?" She slipped the black dress over her head. It was long, slinky, clinging to her curves. "You've been a total ass."

"I know." He leaned back, rested his head against the wall. "I have to be."

"Why? What happened? What changed?"

He looked at her again, a coldness she'd never seen before darkening his eyes. "I have to. And no, I can't explain."

"You can't help me. You can't explain. Fine. That's your business. Just do me a favor. Don't get in my way."

"What are you thinking?"

"You have no right to ask me that."

He stepped forward, took hold of her arms again. "Tell me, Jenny. Damn it, don't you go do something stupid."

"Let me go."

He did, but he didn't step back. "Don't try anything funny, Jenny. Not now."

"Why should I listen to you? You've clearly sold your soul to that bastard."

"Look, you don't have to listen to me. I know that. But do me a favor. Wait. Things are going to change."

"How?"

"I can't say any more. If you love your son, you won't ask me to. All I'm saying is lay low. Let Todd have his way. It won't last forever."

"What are you telling me?"

He turned away from her. "Don't. I've already said too much."

"Too much? You haven't said anything. Damn it, Nick, if not for me, then for my son. Talk to me."

"He won't like that dress," Nick said, eyeing her from shoulder to toes. "It's not slutty enough."

"That's it, then? All you're going to say?"

He reached for the door, but she put her hand on his. "Tell me one thing, all right? Did you feel anything at all for me? Before? When you were in my bed? In me?"

He spun around, took her once more in his painful grip, only this time, his lips came down on hers, hard, bruising, then his tongue was inside, thrusting, and it was as if he wanted to eat her, to devour her.

And there was nothing she could do but give it all

back to him, just as hard, just as desperately. She remembered his taste, the way his lips felt, his tongue teased. The strength of his chest, his shoulders.

She'd memorized him, inch by inch, and it was all so familiar and yet it was all new. Nothing should feel this good and this terrifying.

More.

She wanted more.

He pulled away sharply, looked at her as if she'd tricked him, as if he hadn't been the one to grab her, to kiss her. And then he was outside the dressing room, and the surprised salesclerk gasped, started to complain. Her voice receded until Jenny was alone in the silence, listening to her racing heartbeat, her ragged breath.

None of it made any sense. Patrick in the care of a stranger. Todd with his cruelty and his demands. And Nick, who was the most confusing thing of all.

Chapter Seven

In the two weeks following the incident in the Armani dressing room, Nick made it a point to avoid being too close to Jenny. He had to watch her, although Todd had agreed that not all Nick's time be spent with her. She spent most nights in her own suite, but only after Todd had finished with her. He'd also acquiesced to let her have a few hours every day alone with Patrick. During most of those visits, one of the younger guys who worked with Sweet stayed outside her door, not letting anyone in or out. Except for the days when Nick took Jenny and Patrick out to swim, or to Circus Circus, where Patrick could go on the little kid rides.

Nick wasn't big on children, for the most part. He was the youngest of two, and his older sister and he had been eight years apart, so she was more like an aunt than a sibling.

Nick had never been with a woman who had kids, and he'd never wanted to go there himself, given the kind of life he led. But he liked Patrick. Liked him more than was wise.

He was a corker, that's all. Inquisitive and quick. His laugh was infectious and Nick found himself teasing the boy, making him giggle.

He tried to see the part of Patrick that was Todd, but that probably would come later. When Patrick got a little older, a little more selfish. And when he understood who his father was, what would that be like for him? The money he'd have would soften any blow, that's for sure. But Nick couldn't help thinking the kid might have turned out great if Todd hadn't found him.

Whatever. He had no business getting attached. Things were bad enough with his feelings for Jenny screwing him up but good. Keeping his physical distance was one thing. The woman wouldn't leave his thoughts.

The only thing that chased her away was the very real, very imminent, danger they all faced from Todd. Whenever he wasn't with Jenny or Patrick, Nick was with Todd. He was Todd's liaison to the demolition people who were to implode the El Rio on the Fourth of July.

They'd decided to take the building down at 11:00 p.m. It would give the tourists a chance to witness the implosion then get back to the Strip in time for the midnight fireworks display.

The city was to set off one round at 9:00 p.m., Todd had hired another company for the later celebration. They were expecting nearly three-hundred thousand people on the streets that night, and Nick had to coordinate with the police, the demolition crew and the city planners. Not to mention locate what might end up to be a nuclear weapon, and take Todd down so far he'd never see daylight again.

Todd was flying in a lot of guests for the Fourth, most of them from out of the country, all of them his surveillance equipment customers. Sweet had been given the task of handling those details, and Nick had the feeling that whatever the hell Todd was planning was going to come down with the biggest international audience Todd could assemble.

Nick's boss had doubts about his theory. His boss's boss thought he was barking up the wrong tree, that Todd wouldn't risk his operation just to be a weapon's dealer. Nick knew they were wrong. But he had no proof.

He had the uneasy feeling that proof would come at a cost no one could afford.

It was the second week of June. Which meant, if it was going to break open on the Fourth, that time was running out.

So why in hell did he spend half his waking hours thinking and worrying about Jenny?

At least Nick had determined the layout of the spy equipment in her room. He'd mapped out the safe zones. There weren't many. He'd also tried his sound-neutralization equipment several times and was satisfied it worked. How? Because he was still alive. Simple test, bitch of a pass/fail.

He also knew Jenny hadn't taken his advice to back off. She was up to something. He hoped it wasn't going to get her killed. Because Todd was as enamored of the kid as Nick was. He loved the idea of an heir apparent.

He was grooming the boy to be his successor, and nothing was going to stand in the way. Not Nick. Not Jenny. Nothing.

Nick put away his Palm Pilot and headed back toward Jenny's room. He was supposed to take her shopping yet again, then have her back in time to dress for dinner at eight.

He resented the time spent away from his important work. He resented being a baby-sitter.

He wanted Jenny so badly he could hardly breathe.

AT SIX FEET, three inches, Edward Potereiko towered over his companion as they stood watching the giant cranes load containers onto the *T.R.S.L. Antares*.

"So, Colonel. I suppose this means no more Kalashnikovs?"

Edward's gaze never shifted from the distant workers. "I'm afraid so, Ashida-san. I was never comfortable with it anyway."

Terry Ashida glumly stuck his hands into his pockets. For the past six years he'd bought thousands of surplus AK-47s from Potereiko and resold them for considerable profit on the world markets. The arms trade, and the ready availability of the Russian-made rifles, had made him one of the wealthier men on Hokkaido and a civic leader in Kushiro.

On the positive side, the former Russian army colonel had given him a number of contacts in Russia and the Ukraine, but Terry was not at all confident they would be as honorable in their dealings.

"You look like hell, Potereiko. When was the last time you slept?"

The colonel's gaunt face blocked the sun as he looked down and smiled, exposing a stainless-steel cap. "Days, Ashida-san. Long days. But now I can rest easier. Let me buy you lunch."

Terry met the taller man's smile. "You're buying, Colonel?"

Potereiko shrugged. "Call it friendship. Call it an homage to my new life in a new world. Didn't you tell me you knew the finest seafood restaurant in Kushiro?"

Terry laughed and the two men turned from the fenced-in docks and began walking. "It's on the other side of the Nusamai Bridge," Terry said. "But well worth the walk."

"Just keep it easy. I am tired."

"Why the move, Colonel? If you don't mind my asking."

Potereiko's gait slowed, the bottom of his greatcoat brushing his legs in the sea breeze. He stopped and looked out across Kushiro harbor toward the horizon. "Twenty-five years in the Russian army, and the thanks of a grateful motherland are retirement checks that cannot be cashed. They arrive months late and are too small to live on if they were on time and anyone would honor them."

He met his companion's gaze. "I believe I can sell my knowledge of Russia in the United States, Ashida-san. It's that simple. Today's Russia is a young man's game."

The two men began walking again.

"So why the rush, Edward?"

"I have a job. But I must have my household items in the States by a specific date."

The bridge loomed above them and Potereiko stopped, gazing up at the bronze sculptures that graced the arch. "The four seasons," he said admiringly. "It's a symbol of life itself, yes?"

"A lot of Japanese culture is symbolic," Ashida said. "I think it's in the genes."

"And yet, ultimately everything boils down to life and death, doesn't it, comrade?"

Terry Ashida looked up into Edward Potereiko's eyes and recognized both desperation and irony. "It does indeed, Colonel. Now let's get lunch."

AS SHE WAITED for Nick to show up, Jenny rubbed her arm where Todd had bruised her the night before. She'd put some aloe vera on it; she didn't think it would help. People might notice. Not just people, either. Nick might see.

She shouldn't care. He was the one who had advised her to sit back and do nothing. Thank goodness she hadn't told him her plan. Already she'd managed to stockpile some pretty damning information about Todd's business dealings. She had to be so careful, it was going to take forever to build a case. But tonight, if she played it right, she would have a good opportunity to look through some of his papers.

They were going to a party for a singer who was notorious for the amount of booze, drugs and women at his gatherings. Tonight he was celebrating his fiftieth birthday and, given the occasion, Jenny was sure he'd outdo himself in his excesses. She planned to get Todd drunk. A risky proposition.

After two drinks, Todd was unpredictable. Too little and he just got mean. Meaner than usual, that is. Too much and he got sick, and no one was crankier than Todd when he was sick. Just enough, and he went to sleep for hours. That's what she needed tonight. A few uninterrupted hours to go through his briefcase, his desk. To use the copier without having to watch her back.

He'd actually eased up on her somewhat since she'd been so cooperative. She'd been the perfect little accessory, dressing up for him, waiting on him, fawning over him when they were in public. Of course he'd found new and horrible methods of humiliating her when he could.

She hated it, despised every second of it, but every debasing act fueled her determination to see him put away for life.

Just thinking of what would happen to him in prison made her able to bear about anything. God only knew what he'd do if he ever suspected he wasn't Patrick's father. And if he dreamed Nick was his rival, he'd kill all three of them without hesitation.

Witness protection was her only hope. It would mean never seeing Nick again, but given what he'd become, that was probably a good thing.

Why she couldn't just let him go, let her foolish hopes die, was beyond her ability to understand. She had no idea what he was thinking, if he truly was as devoted to Todd as he appeared, or if he was planning some kind of coup.

It hardly mattered. He'd done his best to keep his distance from her, and he'd never touched her since that day at the Forum Shops.

If only he hadn't kissed her, all of this would have been easier. He'd proved to her that her memories weren't faulty, that his touch electrified her in every possible way. And then to have to see him every day, without any kind of intimacy—

He'd knocked twice, then let himself in. It was nearly noon and she'd had her time with Patrick for the day. Four hours stretched ahead of her like a blank page. Todd had told her to go buy something new to wear tonight, but she didn't want to go shopping. She hated shopping.

She left her bedroom and found Nick standing in the middle of the living room, staring at the new painting that Todd had installed. It was a not-so-subtle reinforcement of who she was, and who Todd was. The lithograph depicted a slave girl being dragged behind a Mongol warrior on a huge horse. Todd had bragged about how many thousands of dollars the piece had cost, but that's not why he'd bought it.

She paused, looking at the man looking at the painting. He wore dark chinos and a retro-looking short-sleeved shirt. The collar was open, the shirt not tucked in. His dark hair was slicked back, and the total picture was utterly striking. He was too good-looking. A man like Nick should be a movie star or a crooner. At the very least, a salesman. He shouldn't be here, with Todd. He didn't make sense with Todd.

He turned to her, raised his eyebrows in an unstated question. The microphones, of course. No words. Big Brother watched. And watched.

"Beautiful, isn't it?"

He didn't move a muscle. Knowing Nick, he'd figured out where the cameras were, and he wouldn't give himself away. Not over a painting. But she could tell he hated it. Hated what it meant. "We're going shopping, yes?"

She nodded. "I need to find something wonderful for tonight's party. Something that will dazzle him."

"Dazzling dresses. I know just the place."

She smiled as if her heart were in it. "I'm ready."

He led her to the door, locked up behind them. Walked her down the hallway, keeping a respectable distance. Not a word, not a glance between them. Yet she felt him as if they were connected by something outside of gravity, outside of science. She practically felt his heart beat in his chest.

It had been like this for days. Whenever he was near, there was a *joining*. Maybe it was because they couldn't speak. Was this how it was in prisons? In wars? Or was it because they had been lovers.

Still wanted to be lovers.

The elevator came. They got in. Silent, vibrating, swimming in this ocean of perception she'd never experienced before.

No, she didn't know what he'd had for breakfast, the color of his boxers. But she knew the ache that lived low and deep inside his chest, all the way through his brain down to his feet. She knew that the not touching consumed him, that he wanted her more than his next breath.

They shared this life on the inside, and she knew with a certainty that if they could speak freely, hold hands, kiss, this awful strain between them would disappear.

It wasn't close to what she wanted, but it was hers and it was all she was going to get. It didn't seem to matter that he'd changed. That he'd gone over to the dark side. That he wouldn't tell her anything.

At the lobby level, he let her out of the elevator first, then followed her to the limo and Kahrim, looking polished as always in his black chauffeur's garb. He helped her into the back seat and they headed off toward the Fashion Show Mall. Two blocks before the turnoff, she looked at Nick, sitting so quietly beside her.

He turned the same second.

Amazing.

She opened her mouth, but he gave a slight, almost-imperceptible shake of his head. As if to prove her point, she realized she'd been about to say something indiscreet, and he, knowing that, had stopped her.

Freaky.

They got to the mall and Nick and Kahrim made their arrangements. Then Nick guided her through the entrance. Once inside, she stopped him. This time he let her speak.

"I can't go to one more store. Not yet. I'm so damn sick of shopping."

He looked around briefly, nodded as if to himself. "There's a coffee shop on the second level. Will that do?"

"That would be wonderful."

He smiled. But only for a second. Then they were walking toward the escalator, still not touching, not talking, even in this public place, because you never knew who was around the next bend, behind the pillar, the elevator door.

He entered the coffee shop first, while she waited. He was back in a moment and they were at a booth, holding menus, the waitress pouring water. Just like real people.

When the waitress left, she sank back, closed her eyes. "God, I'm tired."

"I know," he said, and even his voice was different here. Like the Nick she used to know. "You seem to be settling in."

She opened one eye; stared at him. "Settling in? Is that what you think?"

"I see you with him. How you touch him."

She opened the other eye, not believing what she was hearing. "You're kidding, right?"

Nick reached across the table, grabbing her wrist. She couldn't stop her wince or the fact that he saw it. He let go of her instantly and his gaze shifted to the reddish bruise.

The air seemed to leave him in a whoosh, emptying him until he could hardly hold up his head. "I'm sorry."

"Yeah. Me, too."

"It's because of what I said, isn't it? That you let him—"

"Let him? Like I have a choice?" She leaned over, her gaze never leaving his. "He has my son."

"Yeah." He nodded. "Yeah, he does."

She sat back, then picked up her menu and marveled at the wonders there. Cheeseburgers. Fries. Meat loaf. No pâté, no foie gras, not a piece of endive to be seen.

"You need another minute?"

Jenny looked up at the very ordinary-looking waitress. She smiled. "I know what I want. A cheeseburger, French fries, well-done, please, and a thick, chocolate shake."

"Got it." The woman who was somewhere on the far side of thirty, turned to Nick and gave him a blue-plate smile. "What about you, hon?"

He grinned, but not at the waitress. "I'll have what she's having. Only make my shake vanilla."

Jenny nodded. She knew how Nick watched his diet. Nick lived on egg-white omelets and poached chicken breasts.

"You're a wicked woman, Jenny Granger."

"Yes, I am. And let me tell you something else, Mr. Mason. I intend to have a hot-fudge sundae for dessert. With whipped cream and a cherry. This, despite the fact that I'm having a chocolate shake."

"You maniac. Is there no holding you back?"

"No. Wild horses couldn't stop me."

He laughed. And before she knew it, she laughed, too, and it was the first time she'd laughed in so long that tears came to her eyes, and then she wasn't laughing at all.

He leaned forward, took her hand in his. "Don't. Don't let him take this, too."

She nodded. He was right. This was hers, damn it. Todd couldn't touch her here. Not here, in this dumb little coffee shop with the plastic seats and fake flowers. But the tears, they wouldn't stop.

Not even when Nick got up, walked over to her side of the booth and slipped in next to her. And when he put his arm around her, she was lost.

It didn't stop for a long time. She just cried and cried, and leaned her head on his shoulder. His firm, wide shoulder. She smelled his smell, felt his fingers gentle on her arm. And the tears, they just kept coming.

What stopped them wasn't the milk shakes. It wasn't the cheeseburgers.

What froze the tears in her eyes and the blood in her veins was Henry Sweet, standing on the other side of the coffee-shop door, staring at her and Nick. Lifting a cell phone to his ear.

Chapter Eight

"Damn it." Nick stood just as Sweet disappeared into the mall crowd.

The look on Jenny's face was pure panic. She'd paled and her eyes had grown wide, tears of frustration glistening on her cheeks.

"It's okay," he said, returning to the seat opposite her.

"He saw us, Nick."

Her voice had gone back into the low whisper that characterized all their talks. He hated that damn whisper. "So what? We weren't doing anything."

"No? My head was on your shoulder. Your arm was around me. That's not nothing."

"I'll tell Todd what happened. If we don't make a big deal out of it, it'll be fine."

"What planet are you on? This is Todd we're talking about. He can make a big deal out of a hair clip."

"I can handle it."

He looked at her wrist, the bruise marring her beautiful skin, but more than that, her spirit. She wasn't the Jenny he used to know. Of course she wasn't. Who could live with a monster like Todd and be anything close to normal? It was more than anyone could take.

"I'm an idiot," he said. "Of course, if anyone's going to pay, it's going to be you."

"He doesn't need an excuse," she said. "He just likes them. This will make his night."

"It's not funny."

"No, it's not. But what am I going to do about it?"

"You? Nothing. Me? Plenty."

"Excuse me?"

"Never mind. Eat something. I know how much you wanted that burger."

"Oddly enough, I'm not hungry."

"Screw him. Eat it. Enjoy it. Get your hot-fudge sundae. Get two."

She laughed, although it was without joy. "Yeah. Why not?" She lifted her burger and took a big bite, the lettuce crunch louder than their conversation. He took a huge bite out of his, too, but thoughts of retribution and revenge were the only spices he could taste.

He had to figure out what Todd was planning. And he had to find out damn fast.

Jenny drank her thick shake, her cheeks sucked in with the vacuum pressure. Her color had come back. When she looked up at him, still drinking, her gaze held a curious determination.

"What are you up to, Jenny?"

She lifted her lips from her straw. "Eating. Drinking. Making merry."

"I mean it. I can see you're up to something. Tell me what it is."

"Right. Like I'm supposed to trust you?"

"Damn right you are."

She laughed again. "And I would do that because…?"

"Are you joking?"

"No. Are you?"

"Come on. You know me."

"No I don't. I thought I did, but clearly I was just as wrong about you as I was about Todd."

"Things changed—"

"My point exactly."

"You know that's not what I meant. I've been behaving this way for your own good."

"Gee, thanks."

"I mean it, Jen. I know I've been acting like a jackass, but I have my reasons. I thought you understood that."

"No. I understand nothing. Except Todd has my son. That's the only thing that matters to me in the whole world. He can't continue to have my son. I will do whatever I have to, to make sure he won't."

"That's what I'm worried about."

"Tough."

"You could screw things up for a lot of people."

"Gee, my heart just bleeds for all the other poor folks who aren't being held prisoner in their own homes. I'm just all broken up about them."

Nick rubbed his hand over his face, wishing like hell he knew what to do. His first and only priority was the weapons deal. If Todd was messing with biological or nuclear weapons, it was a threat on an international level. "All right," he said, leaning into the table, taking his voice low enough that she'd have to strain to hear. "I can't tell you everything, but I can tell you something is coming down, and it's coming down soon." He looked behind him, checking to make sure the coast was clear. "Pretty damn soon Sweet's going to be out. And when that happens, things are going to change. I'm gonna make it real clear to Todd that he doesn't get within ten feet of you. Got it?"

"And what on earth makes you think he'll listen to you?"

"I'll have a certain amount of leverage."

"Leverage. And you don't think Todd will kill you the first chance he gets?"

"No. He won't."

She studied him for a long time, her teeth working a small bit of her lower lip.

He doubted she'd bought the tale. A coup within Todd's own organization? He wouldn't have believed it. But she might. She had to. Because he couldn't tell her the truth. Not yet.

"I think there's a way we can help each other," he said, wanting her to stop thinking so hard. "So we can both get what we want."

"What is that you want, Nick?"

"I want my share," he said. "I'm tired of being odd man out. I've done things, Jenny. Things I won't tell you about. But believe me, I'm going to get my due. And when that happens, things aren't going to be easy for C. Randall Todd. Trust me on this."

She shook her head and in that moment he knew she didn't believe him. Jenny was a lot of things, but stupid wasn't one of them.

She sighed. "Fine, whatever. I don't know what you're really up to, and frankly, I don't give a damn. I'm taking care of my own situation, and I expect no help from you or anyone. So let's leave it at that, shall we?"

"But you have access—"

"I have my son. I'm not going to put him at risk, and I'm not going to risk my own life. If I'm not here, who watches out for Patrick, huh?"

"I—"

She put up a hand. "No. I'll pay for my indiscretion tonight. I'll probably pay for a lot more. It won't stop me from what I have to do. Neither will you."

"I can't say that I blame you. Just, please, be careful."

"Yeah. Sure. Careful. Like not letting what we had a lifetime ago make me think there's any reason to trust you."

"That's not what I meant."

"I know."

He leaned back. Closed his eyes. "No, you're right. It's the only way you can think, and survive this." He looked at her again. "Just, somewhere, hold on to the fact that you're not alone. That's all."

"That one thought, Mr. Mason, is more likely to get me killed than anything else. So, no. I won't hold on to that. I can't hold on to that." She put her napkin on the table, scooted out of the booth. "Now I have to buy a dress to wear to a party. And you have to come with me to make sure I don't escape. Let's get on with it."

He almost reached out for her. But he didn't. Because she was right. She was exactly right.

TODD SAID NOTHING about Sweet, about Nick. He told her she looked beautiful in her new dress. He'd kissed her, which made her more nervous than anything else.

She'd been perfect at the party, hardly leaving his side for a moment, smiling at all the right times, laughing at his stupid jokes, touching him just so, letting everyone there see she was his pet, his toy poodle. She'd also fed him what she believed were just the right number of drinks.

Now they were back at the hotel and he was in the bathroom, getting ready for bed. He wasn't all that steady, but she knew there was something that had to be taken care of before he would sleep. And she would see to that, too.

She brushed her hair until it shone, then she sat on the edge of the bed. With no effort, her eyes watered for the full effect. Her hands went to her lap, she cast her eyes down and bowed her head in subjugated repentance.

When he finally came out of the bathroom, he stood in front of her, his broad, flat feet sunk into the plush carpet, toes curling with anticipation.

"What's this?"

"I was bad today, Todd."

"Bad?"

"Yes, sir."

He walked around the bed, but she didn't move an inch. She heard him breathing behind her. "How were you bad?"

"I ate lunch with Nick at a diner at the mall. I got all emotional about something foolish. He came over to make sure I was all right, and I acted like a silly female, weeping all over his shoulder."

"And why is that bad, Jenny?"

"Because I touched him. It was wrong, and I'm sorry."

"You touched him?"

"Yes, sir. His shoulder."

"Is that all you touched?" he asked, moving to stand in front of her once again.

"Yes, sir."

"You didn't perhaps steal a kiss? Take comfort in his bed?"

She looked up then, shock widening her still-damp eyes. "Oh, no. I would never do anything like that."

"No?"

"I belong to you, Todd. Only you."

"That's right. You belong to me."

His voice had gotten louder. A little more slurred.

He took the edge of his finger and put it under her chin, lifting it until she looked into his red-rimmed, boozy eyes. "You touched him even though you know you belong to me."

"I'm sorry, Todd."

"Sorry."

"It won't happen again," she whispered.

"I know it won't. Because we both know the consequences."

"Yes, sir. I understand."

"Do you? Do you know what will happen if you touch him again?"

"You'll kill him."

"That's right. And then…"

"You'll kill me."

"Good girl." He smiled. "You know what to do, don't you, Jenny?"

"Yes, sir."

His right brow rose imperiously.

She let her tears fall again. Giving him just what he wanted. Only this time, they were real.

NICK KNEW WHAT he had to do. He had the weapons and he had the access. He could get into Todd's room, and before security had a chance to get him, he'd blow the bastard's heart out. He'd never make it out alive, but who cared? Jenny would be free and the problem with the weapons would be solved. Maybe.

Damn it, that was the hitch, wasn't it? He wouldn't know if the problem would be solved. The deal might already be in motion. If Todd were out of the picture too soon, things could get messy.

At this point Nick didn't particularly care. He'd heard Todd threaten her one too many times. He couldn't let it go on. Not and live with himself.

But he wouldn't go off half-cocked. He'd make sure

he did things right. He'd call Owen, fill him in. Owen was smart. He'd clean up the mess. Find all the missing pieces.

Then he'd go to Todd's room and take him out.

He got his weapon, made sure he had a full clip. Took another belt of whiskey, although he doubted in his current mood the liquor would affect him at all. Then he got his secure cell and headed out to the elevator. He'd call Owen from the street, away from the hotel. No reason to tip Todd off too soon.

Bastard. Gonna fry.

He got to the lobby, headed for the street. Only he didn't make it. 'Cause his old buddy Henry Sweet popped up right by the front entrance.

Nick stopped. It wasn't a coincidence. Where Sweet was concerned, nothing was by accident.

"You're up late, Nick."

"You, too. Must be tiring, following me around all day."

"Who, me?"

Sweet was an ugly bastard. Broad mug, sunken eyes, bulbous nose broken in who knows how many fights. In the years Nick had known the man, he'd never seen him laugh. He'd smile around the boss, but that was because he had to. The man didn't have normal emotions. And even though Nick had personal knowledge that Sweet had taken care of several men, he'd never seen him get angry. Sweet was the perfect pet. He'd heel, he'd fetch, he'd even kill, all at the snap of Todd's fingers.

"Tell me something, Henry." He hated to be called

Henry. "You ever do anything without Todd telling you to? Anything at all?"

Sweet, his expression placid and unchanging, looked at Nick as if he was a fly on the wall, ready to be swatted. "You don't want to do this, Mason."

"Do what?"

"You don't want to get into it with me." He stepped closer, keeping the conversation private. "I'll snap your neck like a little twig if you mess with me."

"You will, huh?"

"Yeah."

"I don't think so, Henry. You'd have to bother Todd, and Todd's a little busy tonight. You know. Women to hurt and all that."

Sweet's lips curved up in what might have been a grin on a normal person. "Go on up to bed, Nick. You're starting to piss me off."

"What did you tell Todd, huh, Sweet? When you called him from the mall?" He stepped close enough to smell the goon's aftershave. Cologne. Like putting perfume on a toad.

"Just told the man what I saw."

"What you saw was a woman on the edge. You know what he's doing to her."

"It isn't my business what Todd's doing to her. It is my business what you're doing to her."

"That's where you're wrong. She's an innocent, Sweet. Practically a girl. You think it's amusing that he treats her like an animal?"

"Shut the hell up, Mason."

"When are you going to grow a backbone?"

Sweet shook his head, scratched the side of his neck. Nick didn't even see his fist. He just felt his head snap back and then he felt nothing at all.

Chapter Nine

Jenny had to bite back a groan as she slipped out of Todd's bed. He slept, splayed across the bed, exhausted, snoring. He'd fallen asleep almost immediately, which had given her some much-needed respite, but now her heart was pounding as she faced the task ahead of her.

Not even bothering with a robe, she went over to the desk in the corner. She wasn't afraid to move around, as she knew for a fact there were no cameras in here. Todd didn't want any kind of record of his hobbies.

First, she reached far under the desk to retrieve the flashlight she'd taped to the underside this morning. She cursed herself for doing so as the sound of the ripping seemed sure to wake him.

She stood quickly, her hand shaking, her heart loud in her ears, and checked the bed. Nothing had changed, not even the rhythm of his breathing.

His briefcase sat on the desk, closed. After another quick glance at his prone form, she opened the heavy titanium case, not at all surprised by the tidy contents. Todd was a meticulous man. Everything was well ordered in his universe. She had no illusions that the brief-case would turn out to be the mother lode, that every piece was another nail in his coffin.

She put her body between the bed and the flashlight and turned it on. The beam, which was in truth pretty dim, seemed like a klieg light in the darkened room, and it took what felt like forever for her eyes to adjust.

Once they had, she went through the papers in the cen-ter of the briefcase. Some were simple correspondence about the hotel, but others had to do with surveillance or the weapons shows. Anything from or to a foreigner went into the copy stack, which she ordered meticu-lously so that when she put everything back, it would be in the same order as when she'd opened the case.

She kept checking on Todd. He didn't stir, but every second that passed made her more sure that the plan was pure idiocy and that he was too smart to leave anything incriminating in his unlocked briefcase.

She kept on looking, however, because it was all she could do. Finally she reached the bottom of the stack of papers. There was nothing in the upper compartment, but there was a notebook, which she took with her when she slipped out of the bedroom. His office was right next door, and there were no cameras here, either.

The copy machine was on, and loaded with paper. She'd made sure of that this morning when she'd done the bit with the flashlight.

With no concern about neatness, she copied page after page, constantly checking the door, trying to lis-ten above the sound of the machine.

She was shivering now, even though she knew the temperature wasn't the cause. Fear made it hard to breathe, which wasn't helped by her fevered imagination about what Todd would do if he should wake and find her.

When she'd pulled the last piece of paper from the copy machine, she dashed into the bathroom and pulled out her makeup bag. The thick stack barely fit in the tight space, especially with her nervous fingers fumbling so.

After putting the bag under the sink, she retraced her steps, gathered the original documents and opened the bedroom door slowly, peeking in to see if this was going to be her last few minutes of life.

Todd slept on. He'd barely moved an inch and she released a breath she hadn't realized she'd been holding.

She just had to put the stuff back, that was all. A few more minutes and she'd be done.

Her eyes had adjusted well enough that she didn't need to use the flashlight any longer. She turned it off and retaped it to the bottom of the desk. Then she started putting all the papers back, careful to be neat, precise.

She could go to her room as soon as she finished. She opened the flap to slip the notebook back, her heart in her throat. This was crazy, completely nuts. The risk so huge. If he found her out, she'd be dead before sunup. And then what? Patrick would have no one. Just a nanny, but a nanny wasn't a mommy. Mrs. Norris couldn't stand up to Todd. No one could. Patrick would grow up in the shadow of a tyrant. Her sweet baby…what would happen to him? It didn't bear thinking about.

This had to work. They could hide. They'd go somewhere cold. Somewhere with lots of trees and water, far away from anyone who would hurt them. Patrick would be safe. And she would never let anyone humiliate her again.

She closed the briefcase. It looked just as it had before she'd opened it. Now, to get the hell—

"What are you doing?"

Jenny spun around, her hands flying to her chest as her heart nearly burst. Standing in the dim room right in front of the bed, Todd gripped the four-poster as he stared at her through narrowed eyes.

"Nothing."

"Nothing? You had my briefcase."

"I bumped it. I'm sorry. I was just putting it back."

"What were you doing over there?"

"I was coming back from the bathroom."

"Why over there?"

She shook her head, certain he could see her lie, feel her guilt. Every part of her trembled so hard she could hardly keep her balance. "I don't know. I was half-asleep."

He stared at her as she counted the seconds at the end of her life. Patrick. Her most precious gift. Nick. Her greatest regret. She wasn't ready. There were still so many things to be done—

Todd swayed slowly, as if he were on a boat in a rolling sea, and she exhaled with wonder. He was still drunk. Drunk enough that she might live through this. If she played it right.

NICK WOKE in the hell of a headache. His mouth tasted like used cotton, daylight cutting into his eyes with the pain of a laser. Unfortunately he remembered exactly how he'd gotten this way.

He'd been a jerk with Sweet, which was stupid on too many levels to contemplate. And he hadn't killed Todd.

Great. And he was the man standing between the world's safety and C. Randall Todd? Maybe they should all rethink that. He could always find employment in the fast-food industry or perhaps in the janitorial field.

His moan, while expressive, made his head hurt worse, so he shut the hell up as he staggered to the bathroom. After the immediate concerns were taken care of, he faced himself in the mirror and saw the livid bruise on his chin where Sweet's fist had connected.

Touching it, even gingerly with one finger, was not wise, he discovered, so he picked up a toothbrush and toothpaste. Ten minutes and three separate rinses later, he still tasted cotton and aged booze. Abandoning the mint and fluoride, he went instead for coffee, the universal panacea.

There was enough stale coffee in his little pot that he could nuke it. It would taste like hell, but it would take him downstairs to the real coffee in the employee dining room.

He had to get past this headache so he could check on Jenny. Who knows what that bastard had done to her.

"I TELL YOU, Todd, I don't trust him."

Todd leaned back in his chair and stared out across the Las Vegas Valley. The smog was bad, obscuring the view of the foothills. He could see the whole Strip from this seat, watch his fortunes rise as each plane carrying tourist dollars sailed past to land at McCarran. Who said this wasn't a great country? A man from such humble roots as his own could grow up to be richer than his father could have dreamed. His father. A weak man who'd done very few things right in his life. One was to have himself heavily insured. The other was to have been killed in a car crash while on a business trip. Double indemnity. That cash had started Todd on his own road and, whenever he thought of it, he liked to tip his hat to his old man for having the sense to die well.

He thought about Potereiko and his cargo, somewhere in the Atlantic ocean, heading toward California. This deal, this simple transaction, would change everything. He thought about telling Sweet, but no, even Sweet who had proved his loyalty time and again couldn't be trusted with this tidbit. No one knew. Not Potereiko, not the Iraqi buyer, not the Pakistani buyer. No one understood the real beauty of Todd's plan.

The ultimate outcome would be a marvel to behold. The bomb would be sold. Twice. He would end up with well over a billion dollars, safely ensconced in several offshore banks. No one would die, except of course for those most intimately involved.

Then he would turn the bomb over to the authorities, which would make him a hero. Him. He'd save the country. They'd owe him.

"Why, Henry?" Todd spun in a lazy arc to face Sweet. "Why don't you trust him?"

"Because he doesn't respect you."

Todd smiled. He felt more honest affection for the hulking man standing by his Renoir than anyone else in his life, with the possible exception of his son. Surely in time, when Patrick had proven his loyalty, he'd out-shine Sweet considerably. Regardless, Sweet was a good man. A man who knew his place.

But so did Nick. They were opposites, Nick and Sweet, and that was the way he wanted it. Where Sweet was like a bloodhound, Nick was like a fox. They served in contrasting but equally important ways. "It's good that you watch Nick, Henry. But he's still useful to me. Remember that."

"Yes, sir."

"You were right to call me about Jenny. I've taken care of that situation."

"Yes, sir."

"I need you to pick up a man from the airport today, Henry. His name is Tariq Mahmood Ahmad. Don't worry. He speaks excellent English. You'll bring him here. Take him to the Ambassador Suite, and make sure he's comfortable. He'll want to see me, but you'll tell him I won't be available until tomorrow. And make sure, before you go to the airport, that you personally double-check the phone taps in his room."

Sweet nodded. Todd knew he would ask no more questions, except for the time of the Pakistani's arrival. This was a job particularly suited to Sweet. Nick would have asked a great many questions. No, Nick was where he needed to be. His players were all in position.

His only quarrel this morning was with himself. He'd gotten drunk last night, and that was something he couldn't afford to do again. Not until he opened a chilled bottle of French champagne the night his plan came to fruition. A billion tax-free dollars and the thanks of a grateful nation. Quite a legacy to leave his son.

JENNY STUDIED her dresses, unsure what she could wear that would appease Todd. Getting him drunk had worked as far as gaining access to his papers, but he'd been petulant, angry at her instead of himself.

That she'd lived through this morning still shocked her. If Todd had been even a bit more coherent, he'd have seen through her lies. And then? Patrick would have been trapped forever. Alone.

She pulled a dress off the hanger and held it against her body. It was long, powder-blue and covered her back completely. It had a faux turtleneck collar, but the arms were cut out and the way it hugged her body left nothing to the imagination. In fact, her nipples stuck out even if she wasn't cold. God, how could anyone think it was attractive?

She put it back and continued to look, hoping to find something that wouldn't make her cringe.

The thing was, if she was going to continue to put together a case against Todd, she had to think about the consequences if she should fail. Her problems would be over, but what about Patrick?

Maybe she should tell Nick the truth. If he knew Patrick was his, he wouldn't let him stay with Todd. Would he?

No. He might have changed, but surely he could still see that Todd was insane. Besides, the fact that it was Todd would be a secondary issue. Nick wouldn't abandon his own flesh and blood.

Or maybe that was her own wishful thinking. He confused her so much, it was painful to think about him. One minute she believed he was somehow her ally, the next, her enemy. If she told him about Patrick and he was committed to Todd, what then? He might not do anything to rock the boat. Maybe he'd think his son was lucky to have the money and power of Todd behind him. There were simply too many unknowns for her to leave anything to chance. She'd have to stick to her plan, not counting on anyone. However, she'd have to think the fail-safe plan through very carefully. Not do anything rash.

She crossed the closet, wondering if the maids had left the blouse she'd worn on the plane. Jenny thought of her life in Milford, working at the diner. There hadn't been any challenge, except to keep her story from the well-meaning busybodies of the small town, but she'd found a certain grace in doing the simple work to the best of her ability. She had taken comfort in the slow pace of life there, in the town rituals such as the Sunday church supper, the once-a-month bake sale, the football games that the high-school team inevitably lost. She'd created a cocoon for herself and Patrick, and she'd mistakenly thought she could stay there for the rest of her life, or until Todd died, whichever had come first.

But what had really kept her alive, kept her spirit from diminishing beyond hope, were her dreams of Nick. Her fantasies fueled her nights and her days, as she'd spun out one happy ending after another. Her favorite had been a plane crash where only Todd had died. Nick, free from the bonds that had held him to the despot, had searched and searched until one day she'd see him walking into the Hong Kong diner. He'd be tired but when he caught sight of her for the first time, his whole face would light up.

They'd run into each other's arms and, for a long time, they'd say nothing. Just hold each other tight, breathe in the closeness, revel in the love that had swelled and deepened with each passing day.

She'd take him to pick up Patrick and he'd know, that first instant, that it was his son he was seeing. He'd feel a bond as strong as destiny and he'd tell her he'd never leave them again. They'd be a family, the three of them, forever.

She had to laugh at her naiveté, or else she'd weep and never stop. Todd certainly wasn't dead, and even if that had been true, Nick wouldn't have come searching for her. Clearly he'd hardly thought of her at all during the nearly three years they'd been apart. As for the bond with Patrick?

He liked the boy. But who wouldn't? Patrick was an amazing kid who could charm the birds from the trees. But the hoped-for connection between them was nothing more than wishing on a star.

Ah, the blouse. Washed, ironed. Someone, unknowing, had preserved this tiny bit of her old self. Ironic how she longed for a life she'd so bitterly resented. Now it seemed a paradise.

Money. It was the cause of it all. She'd never considered herself money hungry. She hadn't dreamed of it, except in the usual sense. But she'd been seduced as if she'd grown up without a penny. It wasn't the baubles or even the cachet that had got her. It was the beauty.

In the beginning, Todd'd bought her nice things, gorgeous things. Not the gaudy crap he'd forced her to wear. There'd been this one necklace, just a simple teardrop diamond with a platinum chain, and it had been exquisite.

And then there was that time he'd found her reading about Michelangelo and the following week he'd taken her to Florence, Italy. They'd lunched at Pandemonia and she'd spent a whole afternoon in the stunning presence of David.

She'd been bought, that's all. Just like the call girls in the casino. Only she'd charged more. Now there's something to be proud of.

The blouse felt like an old friend. She knew she wouldn't be able to wear it for a long time, but the next few hours would feel like a luxury. Clothed, covered, her shame hidden. It was the best she could hope for.

Instead of jeans she pulled out a pair of shorts, white, also, that weren't too tiny or too tight. And none of those awful shoes with suicide heels, either. Bare feet. Yeah.

She wiggled her toes in the carpet, looked at her reflection in the mirror, and for once didn't feel like wincing.

A long time ago she'd been a normal girl. Maybe she could be a normal woman, someday. It didn't matter if she had a different name. An address she couldn't imagine. Freedom existed and she was going to find it again for herself and her son.

It was early still, and she had an hour or so to go before she could see Patrick. Coffee would be nice. She could read. Definitely take some aspirin for the tension in her back and shoulders. Try not to worry. As if that was a possibility.

She turned out the light and reached for the door, but it swung open, sending her heart into her throat. Jumping back, she held back a gasp when Nick, not Todd, stepped just inside.

His finger went to his lips, but it was the look in his eyes that quieted her much more effectively.

She didn't even dare ask what was wrong. She just tried to remember how to breathe as she waited for him to tell her what was going on.

"Go back in. Change into something else. Take your time."

He'd whispered so quietly she'd had to strain to hear, but she didn't hesitate after she'd understood. She just went back to the center of the closet, next to the low velvet chair, and unbuttoned her blouse, one slow button at a time.

She couldn't tell exactly what Nick was doing, because she only saw him in her peripheral vision. He'd slunk against the wall, taken something from his jacket pocket. Then he'd turned his back, working feverishly at something behind the hanging rod.

Once her blouse was off, she reluctantly hung it back up, then got another shirt, this one with no sleeves and a size smaller, and slipped it on, again, taking her time with the buttons. By the time she had finished, so had Nick. He stood, breathing hard, staring at her from the side of the closet.

"It's okay," he said, his voice still low, but not that bare whisper.

"What did you do?"

"I fixed the camera," he said. "We're safe in here now."

"What about the microphones?"

"Already taken care of. But don't do any shouting."

"The whole closet is safe?"

He nodded. "The whole closet."

"Unless Sweet decides to pay a visit."

"Ah, but I've thought of that, too. If anyone comes into the suite, my pocket will vibrate. I've set up a motion detector and it will set off the alarm on my pager."

"Wow. Handy gadget."

"Yeah. I lent it to one of the women upstairs. She kept calling for room service."

Jenny laughed. But her laughter stilled as Nick moved in closer.

What she saw in his gaze wasn't the least bit humorous.

Chapter Ten

Her laughter faded as Nick moved closer. Then there wasn't anything to hear but breathing. She'd been on his mind all morning, even when he'd met with Owen.

His boss had told him that they had identified a Pakistani radical coming in to the Henderson airport, on Todd's private plane. They wanted to pick him up, which would be a huge mistake. Nick did agree that more surveillance on all of Todd's properties was a wise move, but to mess with what he had going could blow everything sky-high, in the most literal sense. But Owen had also had the equipment Nick had asked for, so their meeting wasn't all frustration.

He'd finished with Owen, come back to the hotel and, after a quick shower, had come right down, his thoughts a constant stream of conflicting emergencies. Todd. Sweet. The Pakistani. Bombs. Jenny, Jenny, Jenny.

And here she was, standing close enough that he could smell the hint of citrus in her hair. There was nothing to do but touch her, let his fingers land gently on her shoulder, urge her forward.

She came willingly, her gaze as familiar as his dreams. He leaned down those few inches, touched the soft cream of her lips with his own.

Jenny sighed and he tasted her need.

He pulled her in tight. But she was tense, all the muscles in her back as taut as bow strings.

"Jenny, I can leave."

She shook her head. "I'm okay," she said in the whisper he heard every time his eyes closed.

"You're not. You're scared to death."

"Of course I am. And you should be, too. But I don't care. I need to forget. To make him disappear."

"Ah, Jenny," he said.

She didn't say anything at all, and he lost her. Her gaze slipped away, staring past him, past the safety of the closet to the terror of out there.

No. He'd gotten a film loop of the closet to the boys outside and they'd rigged it so that whoever the hell was doing the surveillance wouldn't know they were there. He'd fixed the microphones himself, so all they would hear was white noise.

This was all he could do. This stupid room with the racks and racks of shoes and rows of clothes and hats and purses, and the ugly velvet chair. But there were also the big pillows and the thick carpet, and they could make themselves a little nest, and he could touch her and feel her pale, cool palm on his hot, thick flesh.

He'd get her back. Gently. Carefully. Take her away. Bring her home.

He touched the side of her cheek with his fingers and

Jenny looked up. There he was again, the one she recognized, the one she'd loved and never stopped loving. The man she wasn't sure was real.

"I'm here," he whispered. "Right now."

"Who are you?"

His lips curved up on one side with the smile that had been her downfall. She was a strong woman and had trained herself to stand tough when everything told her to fold. But when it came to that smile, the way the lines spread from the edges of his eyes, the way his forehead furrowed, the cleft in his chin…the whole damn package, she was helpless. She'd wait forever for that smile.

"I'm Nick," he whispered. "You know me. Just like I know you." He leaned a bit to his right and kissed the curve of her neck, making her tremble. "I know you're ticklish right here." Then he took her earlobe between his teeth, nibbled long enough to weaken both her knees and her resolve. "I know the shape of your nose, how your skin feels after a bath. I know how you taste, Jenny. Every part of you. And I'm so damned hungry, I can't stand it."

She took in a deep breath of the masculine scent that was Nick and no one else on earth. Then she raised her arms and curled her hands around his neck. She kissed his chin, then closed her eyes. "I remember you, too," she said. "Everything. Every move, every word, every touch."

"Yes," he said. "Everything."

"More," she said. "Give me more to remember."

"Exactly what I had in mind."

His hands moved down her back in a caress so gentle it took her breath away. And when those same hands moved to the front of her body and peeled back her shirt, he took far more than her breath.

TODD HUNG UP the phone and turned to face Sweet. "Well?"

"He's settled, sir. He asked when he could see you. He seemed nervous."

"I would imagine. I'll see him when I'm ready. When he's had time to sweat."

"I told him, sir."

"Good. And no one saw you?"

"No, sir. There was no tail. No one at the airport. I took the Pakistani in the back way. It was private."

"Excellent." Todd walked over to his desk, glanced at his calendar. "There's been a change of plans for tonight. I'll be going to the opening of the new review at the Mirage. On your way out, tell Jenny she'll need to be ready at six. And tell her to wear the gold dress."

"Yes, sir. She's in her room?"

Todd sat in the chair he'd had specially made from kid leather. He swiveled to his right and pressed a button on his desk. A panel on the far wall lowered slowly, revealing a bank of television monitors. He glanced from screen to screen, searching her bedroom, her living room, her kitchen, even her bath. The suite was empty and silent. No activity in her closet or in the spare room. He looked at his Rolex and frowned. "Find out where she is, would you, Sweet? And get back to me."

"Yes, sir." Sweet, ever the obedient servant, turned to leave. As he got to the office door, Todd cleared his throat.

"And find Nick for me, would you? His cell phone seems to be on the blink."

Henry Sweet smiled. "Be happy to, sir."

JENNY FELL.

And Nick was there to catch her.

Like stepping off a curb, turning on a light, blinking. That's how easy it felt to let go. She put all the worry and trouble and truth somewhere outside. Inside, she gave herself to her lover. She smiled as his fingers traced the underside of her breasts, as his mouth left her lips and circled her nipple. Her head went back, resting on a cushion so large it was like a cloud, and her eyes closed so that the outside moved farther away.

His moan, guttural, low, like the growl of a lion, belied his slow movements, his achingly gentle touch. Her hand went to his head where with spread fingers she raked the thick dark mane, pressing him closer.

He moved away, leaving her breasts exposed, wet, tightly budded against the air from the ceiling vent. Lifting her head, she saw him take off his shirt, toss it to the side of the pillow, then he unclasped his belt, snapped it back, ripped down his zipper. Spurred by his action, she pushed her shorts down, taking with them the terrible white thong panties. She shoved them down her legs, kicked them so high they landed on the velvet chair.

But she didn't care, because he was naked, his chest

An Important Message from the Editors

ear Reader,

, you'd enjoy reading romance novels with larger print hat's easier on your eyes, let us send you TWO FREE HARLEQUIN INTRIGUE® NOVELS in our NEW LARGER-PRINT EDITION. These books are complete and unabridged, but the type is set about 25% bigger to make it easier to read. Look inside for an actual-size sample.

By the way, you'll also get a surprise gift with your two free books!

Pam Powers

l off Seal and
Place Inside...

LARGER-PRINT
FREE BOOKS
EDITION

THE RIGHT WOMAN

she'd thought she was fine. It took Daniel's words and Brooke's question to make her realize she was far from a full recovery.

She'd made a start with her sister's help and she intended to go forward now. Sarah felt as if she'd been living in a darkened room and some- one had suddenly opened a door, letting in the fresh air and sunshine. She could feel its warmth slowly seeping into the coldest part of her. The feeling was liberating. She realized it was only a small step and she had a long way to go, but she was ready to face life again with Serena and her family behind her.

All too soon, they were saying goodbye and Sarah experienced a moment of sadness for all the years she and Serena had missed. But they ad each other now and that's what

She held

PRINTED IN THE U.S.A.
Publisher acknowledges the copyright holder of the excerpt from this individual work as follows:
THE RIGHT WOMAN Copyright © 2004 by Linda Warren. All rights reserved.
® and TM are trademarks owned and used by the trademark owner and/or its licensee.

YOURS FREE!
You'll get a great mystery gift with your two free larger-print books!

GET TWO FREE LARGER-PRINT BOOKS!

YES! Please send me two free Harlequin Intrigue® romantic suspense novels in the larger-print edition, and my free mystery gift, too. I understand that I am under no obligation to purchase anything, as explained on the back of this insert.

PLACE FREE GIFTS SEAL HERE

199 HDL D4AU   399 HDL D4AV

FIRST NAME	LAST NAME

ADDRESS

APT.#	CITY

STATE/PROV.	ZIP/POSTAL CODE

Are you a current Harlequin Intrigue® subscriber and want to receive the larger-print edition?

Call 1-800-221-5011 today!

◄ **DETACH AND MAIL CARD TODAY!** ▼

(H-ILPI-03/05) © 2004 Harlequin Enterprises Ltd.

The Harlequin Reader Service™ — Here's How It Works:

Accepting your 2 free Harlequin Intrigue® larger-print books and gift places you under no obligation to buy anything. You may keep the books and gift and return the shipping statement marked "cancel." If you do not cancel, about a month later we'll send you 6 additional Harlequin Intrigue larger-print books and bill you just $4.49 each in the U.S., or $5.24 each in Canada, plus 25¢ shipping & handling per book and applicable taxes if any.* That's the complete price and — compared to cover prices of $5.24 each in the U.S. and $6.24 each in Canada — it's quite a bargain! You may cancel at any time, but if you choose to continue, every month we'll send you 6 more books, which you may either purchase at the discount price or return to us and cancel your subscription.

*Terms and prices subject to change without notice. Sales tax applicable in N.Y. Canadian residents will be charged applicable provincial taxes and GST.

broad, perfectly muscled, with dark hair curling around his nipples, swirling along the center of his chest down his stomach. Blossoming again where his thick length rose arrogant and ready.

He was more beautiful than she remembered, more chiseled and toned. His thighs. She wanted to touch them, to feel the strength beneath the tanned flesh.

He had his own plans, though, covering her body with his.

She readied for his kiss, but it didn't come and she blinked to see him struggling with something in his pants' pocket. For a wild second she thought it was a gun, then she saw the silver packet and she relaxed. She opened her mouth to tell him the condoms hadn't worked the last time, but he swooped down and captured the words on his wicked tongue.

He arched over her, kissing her, but not lying on her. It took her a moment to realize he was being exceptionally tender, and another part of her heart went out to him. She solved the dilemma by turning on her side. He let himself sink into the pillow, curl his long leg over her thigh, his hands stroking, exploring. His lips tasting, sucking, licking. Making her wet and needy.

Her hand slid down the delicious planes of his chest and stomach until she found his length. Circling him with her hand earned her a gasp and a significant curse. She laughed, but only until he kissed her silent.

Then she stroked him and he moved his talented fingers to the juncture of her thighs, where he petted the soft lips, bare, smooth and swelling even as he touched her.

When he slipped inside her, she arched back, pushing him in quickly, wanting him to work his magic. She remembered how he touched her.

Even though she knew they wouldn't be overheard, the habit was so ingrained that she kept her gasps low, her moans discrete, and transferred all that energy inside, into their secret.

He tore open the condom, slipped it on, and then, to save him from having to make the decision, she pushed him onto his back and straddled him. He held himself ready and she sank down slowly, head thrown back, mouth open, chest heaving as she felt him fill her inch by incredible inch. And then she was home and he was in her, and they weren't two people anymore, but one. One panting creature, met in a union of bliss.

All the world was away, out there. The only thing that existed was her, was him, was them, and the friction as she slowly rose and fell, impaling herself, rubbing her sweet spot just so…

His hands on her hips, his face gorgeous even when it was all contorted and controlled. She laughed, the only sound aside from snatched breath and stifled moan.

Another second. Another. The pace quickened, his hips thrust up while she pounded down. A rhythm so fine, so theirs, they didn't need gravity.

Once more, and she cried out. Not loud, oh, no. A silent cry at the thundering climax that shook her body from head to toe, from fingers to eyelashes. She climbed, climbed, and there was the peak, where there was no Todd, no Xanadu, no fear, no pain. Just Nick and unbearable pleasure.

When she finally breathed again, he still strained, pushing into her as if he could bury himself there forever, his face a mask that looked as fierce as the leopards on the tapestries that hid the cameras in the living room.

She gasped for breath as he let the air out of his lungs in a great whoosh. Her body fell forward and he caught her, held her tight.

For the first time since that awful morning, she felt whole and safe. The truth was just out the door, but the door was still shut. And she could hold on to her dream for another breath, another sigh.

Her gaze was caught by his shirt, by something odd. She wanted to close her eyes, to stay in that sweet never-never land, but she couldn't, and she focused.

His shirt moved, vibrated, as if it wanted to come to life. With rubbery arms, she forced herself up to see the disappointment in Nick's face. "Look," she whispered.

He turned, awkwardly, with her still on him. He saw the shirt and a second later she felt his whole body stiffen as if he'd been shocked with a hundred volts.

Still gentle, but firm and serious, he lifted her up until she found her feet. "Someone's here."

All the joy left her body in a flash and she hunted for her shorts, crammed into them, while Nick dressed in seconds.

"What if it's Todd?"

"It'll be okay."

"It won't," she said. "He'll kill us."

"It's not Todd. It's probably a maid."

"She'll tell him. They all report to him."

"She won't know anything's wrong. I swear."

"What are you going to say?"

"I don't know yet."

"God, Nick. Please. Not like this."

He got her blouse from the floor, dressed her as if she were a child. Then he buttoned her up, which was good because her fingers shook so badly, she never could have done it herself.

"You stay here. I'll go out. See who it is." He kissed her, hard, on the lips. "Don't worry."

She nodded.

He ran a hand through his hair, straightened his shirt. Then he went to the door.

"Nick."

He stopped, looked back at her.

"I love you."

He closed his eyes. But only for a moment. When he looked at her again, he was already outside. His body followed and she managed to get to the velvet chair before she collapsed.

It was too much. Too much of everything, and she wanted off. She cradled her head in her hands and while she felt as though she could cry forever, no tears came. Just sadness. More sadness than should have been in the whole wide world.

ALTHOUGH THE PORTS of Hong Kong and Singapore were perennial favorites, Edward Potereiko liked Long

Beach because it was so clean and direct. Dedicated to container shipping with virtually no fishing industry and few marinas, Long Beach presented a relatively fresh face to the casual visitor.

Additionally, most of the necessary government offices and many shipping companies were within a two- or three-mile radius, easy hiking distance for a sixty-year-old man who had walked his whole life.

At 301 East Ocean, the retired colonel stood at the Customs desk on the eighth floor, patiently waiting while the inspector, an attractive woman in her mid-twenties, dealt with the couple in front of him. Potereiko gave her his broadest smile as he stepped forward with his passport and a sheaf of shipping documents.

"Good afternoon, Inspector…Rodriguez," he said, reading her name tag. "I hope I said that correctly."

She rewarded him with a smile of her own. "Better than a lot of people here. What can I do for you—" she quickly scanned his passport "—Mr. Petrov?"

"I have taken a temporary job in Las Vegas. It will last about a year, and I have brought some personal items with me." He slid the documents across to her.

She leafed quickly through the Russian passport, noted his temporary work visa, and checked over the shipping documents. "Can you wait a few minutes, Mr. Petrov? I have to look up the manifests on the computer."

"Certainly."

She headed for a nearby desk with the passport and documents.

Potereiko smiled inwardly. His passport in the name

of Ivan Petrov had indeed been issued by the Soviet government to allow him to travel anonymously while he was still in the army. It was one of several things he had kept when he retired.

Ten minutes later Inspector Rodriguez returned. "Everything seems to be in order, Mr. Petrov. I see Tiger Shipping is acting as your broker?" She tapped her finger on the documents.

"That is correct."

"And you've indicated you're bringing in a single crate with household items worth less than two thousand dollars?"

Potereiko laughed out loud. "It wouldn't be worth that without the laptop. A favorite desk and chair, a computer. A few books."

"Is that some kind of Russian computer, sir?"

"Toshiba." He was still grinning.

She returned his smile. "Yeah, I love mine." She pulled a handful of stamps from a drawer and began stamping the various documents. "Okay, tell Tiger to ship your belongings to Las Vegas under a Customs seal. It'll get there faster and the local Customs office can clear your belongings." She swept the stamps back into the drawer and picked up his documents and passport. "Welcome to America, Mr. Petrov."

"The land of opportunity, Inspector."

Chapter Eleven

No one was in her bedroom, which gave Nick another few moments to figure out what he was going to say if it was Todd. He'd jammed his phone, which would give him something of an excuse. He'd have to say they'd just gotten back in case Todd had looked at the surveillance tapes.

He walked past the second bedroom, glancing inside. No one. The kitchen was empty, too. When he turned the corner to the living room, his suspense ended. Sweet, looking like the cat who ate the canary, stood leaning against the wall next to the slave-girl painting.

"Gee, now who would have thought I'd find you here?" Sweet said. "When the boss just gave the whole place a little look-see and no one was home?"

"What do you want, Henry?"

"Jenny."

"Why?"

"What the hell difference does it make to you?"

"I'm looking after her."

Sweet pushed himself off the wall. "You are, huh?"

"Yeah."

"I think Todd will find that a real interesting comment."

"Why? He's the one who put me in charge."

"Yeah, well from the cheap seats, it still looks like Todd's in charge of Jenny. You're just a baby-sitter."

"Just tell me what Todd wants and get out."

"Where's Jenny?"

"She's—"

"Right here."

Nick swung around to see Jenny walk into the living room looking cool and collected. Not at all like a woman who'd just made love. Her hair was silky smooth around her shoulders, her lips red and glossy. Her clothes looked fresh and pressed. She was stunningly beautiful and he wanted to drag her right back into the closet.

Sweet looked from Jenny to Nick, then back again. "Mr. Todd was looking for you."

"Yes?" she said, for all the world like the mistress of the castle to a lowly footman.

Sweet cleared his throat. "He asked that you be ready at six. In the gold dress."

"Is that all?"

"He'll want to know where you were."

"I'll tell him at six."

Sweet squared his shoulders and Nick could almost see him switch into commando mode. "That won't do. I have to tell him when I go back."

Jenny pursed her full lips as she stared hard at Sweet. "You may tell Mr. Todd that I was with Nick, as ordered. I accompanied him to his room for a moment."

Sweet's brows rose.

"My phone crapped out," Nick said, stepping closer to Jenny. "I had to get my spare."

Henry didn't care for the response; at least, his scowl indicated displeasure. Nick relaxed. Sweet would have been smug as hell if he had something concrete he could take to Todd.

"So unless there's something else?" Jenny said.

The big man didn't answer for a moment. He wanted to bust them. To make Nick look bad. He didn't care one whit if that would earn Jenny another night of hell.

Henry was going down. Right after his boss.

"I'll tell him. I don't think he'll be real happy about you going to Nick's room."

"You can tell Mr. Todd we were there for approximately three minutes. Then we came back. I can't imagine anyone thinking there was anything inappropriate about it. But feel free to exaggerate if you must." Jenny walked right up to him. The top of her head reached the bottom of his chin. She didn't let that stop her. "I know you crave those brownie points, Henry. Tell me, is there a Jenny merit badge? Or would it be a Nick Mason badge?"

Sweet's pasty face turned pink, especially his cheeks. "Tell you something, missy," he said, his voice low and menacing. "You're expendable. It's the boy who matters, not you. So I'd be careful if I was you."

"If I were you, I'd commit suicide," she said.

Nick bit back a laugh while he made sure he could get to his gun. He didn't think Henry would go off, but he'd be ready.

"He'll get tired of playing with you," Henry whispered. "And when he does, he won't give a damn what I do to you."

"I'm breathless with anticipation," she said. "Now, please. Go. Tell Todd I'll be ready at six."

Henry breathed so heavily Nick could see his nostrils expand and contract. But he didn't say any more. He just turned and headed for the door. As he passed Nick, he bumped his shoulder, forcing Nick into the side of the end table. It hurt, but Nick didn't make a sound. He just smiled real pretty.

Henry slammed the door when he left.

Jenny sagged, but then she must have remembered she wasn't in the clear. That every move was being recorded. "I swear," she said, turning to Nick, "the man lives for drama. I can't believe he'd be upset about us getting your phone."

"He's just doing his job."

"I suppose."

"We've got a few hours before you have to be ready. Anything you want to do?"

"If I can, I'd like to see Patrick."

"I'll check with Mrs. Norris. Sit tight."

It wasn't easy to walk out of the room as if they had just gone to change his phone battery. He wanted to touch her, to finish the long, slow, sweet time of coming down, of holding each other, whispering secrets and lies. But they didn't get to have that slice of normal. Instead he had to go ask permission for Jenny to see her son for an hour before she had to dress like a call girl for the sickest bastard in America.

He closed the door behind him and walked the short distance to the nanny's room. He had to wait a minute for Mrs. Norris to answer the door, and when she did, she was holding Patrick. The kid saw Nick and his face lit up as if he'd seen Santa or the Easter Bunny.

When Mrs. Norris held him out, Nick took him. It was weird, because the only other kid he'd held was his niece, Sarah, who'd been about three. She'd stiffened and screamed so loud he thought he'd need hearing aids. Needless to say, Sarah had gone to her mother and Nick had stayed the hell away from toddlers.

Only, Patrick didn't have that reaction at all. He grabbed on to Nick's neck, yelling, "Nick, Nick!" so loud he'd wake the neighbors, if they'd had any.

"Well, you certainly have a friend, don't you?"

"I guess," he said. "Don't know why."

"Nick!"

Smiling, Nick looked into the boy's dark eyes, so inquisitive and eager. "How you doin', kiddo?"

"I made pizza!"

"You did?"

Patrick nodded so hard his hair flopped up and down. "With cheese."

"Wow. That must have been great."

"I spilled 'matos all over the floor."

"Oops. I bet that made a mess."

Patrick nodded again. "Mrs. Norris says I'd try a staint."

"A 'staint,' huh?"

"Yeah."

Nick grinned, looked up to see Mrs. Norris smiling right back.

"And know what else?"

"What?"

Patrick held his hands out as wide as he could. "Mrs. Norris loves me this much."

"That's a whole lot."

"But not as much as Mommy."

"Right. No one can love you as much as Mommy can. And you know what?" He raised his gaze to the nanny. "She'd love to come see you right now."

Patrick shouted and Mrs. Norris nodded. When Nick turned to go tell Jenny, he saw he didn't have to. She was standing just behind him. Crying.

He went to hand the kid back, but Patrick caught sight of Jenny, and that was all they wrote. He was in her arms in a flash and Jenny was wiping tears as she laughed and marveled at his pizza adventure.

What the hell were they doing in this freak show? These were good people. Decent. Normal. The last people on earth that should be caught up in the end of the world.

But then, that's why he needed to stop Todd, wasn't it? Because of Jenny and Patrick. And all the Jennys and Patricks and Mrs. Norrises out there.

So the lesson here was simple. Keep his pants zipped, his hands to himself and stop the madman next door from sending them all to the great beyond. There were still things that needed to be done here.

Patrick needed to grow up. Jenny needed to be happy.

TODD SEEMED in a particularly good mood, which Jenny was going to spoil if she didn't get with the program. He'd taken her to one of his favorite restaurants, Papillion, at the top of Le Mystique, one of his smaller hotels. It would have been nice to go somewhere he didn't own and everyone didn't kiss his butt, except that would be asking for the moon.

She had to admit, the meal was fantastic. She'd had a goat cheese and balsamic salad, then a filet mignon that was extraordinary. Everything was the best, the most, the finest. As was the view. She could see the entire Strip from her seat, aglow in the magic of neon and moonlight. It really was beautiful, if you just looked at it as color and light. As hard as she tried, though, she couldn't quite forget the facade. Just like she couldn't forget the handsome man across from her wasn't a man at all. She couldn't have said exactly what he was, except that he wasn't human.

Todd sipped some Scotch, ate a piece of his steak. Behind him, a gloved waiter, a sommelier and the maître d' hovered, waiting for him to lift his finger, at which point they would appear at the side of the table as if conjured from a magic lamp. It must be traumatic for him to have to go to the bathroom for himself.

"I've been thinking about my boy's education," he said.

She didn't cringe. In fact she smiled, looked interested and eager to hear his thoughts.

"Military school is the way to go. He needs to understand discipline, honor, duty. Then to prep school. Andover. Or Choate. I don't know yet."

"That's a good plan for later, Todd. But you know, he's not even ready for kindergarten yet."

"I'm having an early childhood specialist come in to see him twice a week. He'll be reading before he's four."

"Do you think it's a good idea to push so hard when he's so young?"

Todd's smile shifted, and she got it. She was the one who'd pushed too far and she'd better backtrack—fast.

"On the other hand, he is so special. I'm sure he's aching to read."

"Yes. That's right. He wants to perform, I can see that in him. I was like that when I was a child. Reading before I hit the age of three. My parents, they didn't have a clue what to do with a child with my capabilities. The smartest thing they could have done was to find me parents who knew what they were doing, and sign me over."

"But look at you now. It seems to me everything turned out perfectly."

He smiled at her, this one as genuine as he could manage. "That's very astute. I like that, Jenny. Very much."

"Just telling it the way I see it," she said.

He nodded, happy with her fawning, happy knowing his son was just like him.

She put her napkin on the table. "Please excuse me," she said, standing. "I have to go to the ladies' room."

"Wait a minute," he said as he reached into his pocket and pulled out his money clip. He handed her a fifty.

"Thank you," she said. "I won't be long."

He looked pointedly at his watch. "Don't be."

She kissed his cheek, then hurried to the back of the

restaurant. The whole way there she kept her smile in place, her bearing as regal as she knew how. When she went in to the lavishly appointed ladies' lounge, there were two women there, so she barreled through to the bathroom and locked herself in a stall.

Her face crumpled before she did and she found herself sitting on the commode, pressing her fingers on her closed eyelids so she wouldn't cry. She couldn't cry.

Seeing Patrick in Nick's arms had been the last straw. Making love with him had knocked her for a loop, but when she'd seen him with their baby...

The tears wouldn't be held back. They came, hot and plentiful down her cheeks, dripping onto the twenty-thousand-dollar pale gold dress.

This was not good. She couldn't come out of the bathroom looking as though she'd lost her best friend. She hadn't even brought her purse, so there went any chance of fixing her makeup.

No, that wasn't true. This was Papillion. The rest room had an amenity bar. There was perfume and hair stuff, and if there was any mercy in the world, the attendant would also have some makeup.

As for Nick and Patrick, they would have to wait. She wasn't about to think of them here, in this toilet. Or out there, with that horrible man. They deserved the best she could give them.

Tonight, when she'd been excused, she'd curl up in bed and she wouldn't sleep for hours and hours. She'd remember every second of her time with Nick. She'd picture the two of them together. At least in her bed, under her covers, she could have some joy.

She blew her nose, patted her cheeks and walked out of the stall. After she washed her hands, she went around to where the attendant sat in her starched uniform. Mercy was present in the form of pressed powder, mascara and rouge. Not exactly in her colors, but Jenny didn't care.

She took pains fixing the damage, and when she was finished, she gladly handed the nice woman the fifty-dollar bill. Then she went back for round two, with firm determination not to think of her men until she was alone.

Todd looked at his watch when she got back, and he didn't seem upset. It could all be an act, of course. She'd find out later. One thing about Todd, he liked to enumerate her sins, real or imagined.

"You look beautiful," he said as the waiter held her chair for her.

"Thank you. I want to make you proud."

"You do, my love. When you're good, you're very, very good."

"And when I'm bad?"

"You're punished."

Her smile froze on her lips, but he thought it was hilarious. She laughed along with him and ordered a second Scotch.

Todd called the waiter and whispered something to the young man, who bowed, then disappeared. Todd turned back to her. "I visited Patrick today."

Jenny's blood grew cold. "Oh?"

"He's one hell of a scrapper, that boy. Good set of lungs."

"He can be quite, uh, loud."

"Huh. I was somewhat concerned about a few things."

"What are those?"

"First, I asked him to call me Daddy. He won't."

"He'll learn, Todd. He's just a baby." ·

Todd grunted. "What about that thing on his back."

Jenny swallowed. She hadn't wanted Todd to see it. God, how she hadn't wanted that. "It's a birthmark, that's all. It doesn't hurt him."

"I want it removed."

"The doctor said it was perfectly harmless—"

"We'll have it removed. I don't want him having any deformities."

"I understand."

He smiled again. "Did he show you what I brought him?"

"No, he didn't. But I didn't have much time with him today."

"I'm sure you'll see it tomorrow. It's a fire truck. Large. Perfectly to scale. I special ordered it for him last week."

"That was very kind, Todd."

"He's my son. He'll have everything."

"I know," she said.

"Including parents who are married."

Her fork clattered to the table as the waiter reappeared, only not with a glass of Scotch but a bottle of French champagne. Her heart nearly stopped when

Todd pulled out a blue-velvet box and opened it, so slowly she wanted to scream.

The diamond was pink, and it was a monster. She had no concept of how many carats it could be, but she doubted she'd be able to lift her hand once it was on.

"Are you surprised?"

"Yes. Very."

"You didn't think I'd forgiven you, did you?"

"No, Todd, I didn't. I thought…"

"You thought I wouldn't want you back, after you left the way you did. After you abandoned me. And then, when I found out you'd had our child and never even called—"

"Todd, I'm sorry about that. I was wrong."

"Yes, you were. And I have no doubts you'll never do anything like it again."

"No, never."

"Give me your hand."

She willed herself not to shake as she reached across the table. He put the thing on, a marquis so big it looked like something from a museum, or a joke shop. But she knew it was real. He'd never buy anything that wasn't the best.

"It's the largest pink diamond in the world."

"It's stunning, Todd," she said as she brought it close to examine it. "I'm speechless."

"I would think so. It's worth over four hundred thousand dollars a carat. That's over eight million dollars on your finger."

"Oh, God, Todd. What if something happens to it? I'd be afraid to wear it."

"You'll wear it. And it will be safe."

"But—"

"It will be safe," he repeated, so forcefully that she knew there would be no more discussion. "The wedding will be on the Fourth. We won't have many guests. But you'll wear that ring and a wedding band when we take down the El Rio. Nothing will ever be the same after that night, let me tell you. Nothing."

"I know, Todd. I know."

Chapter Twelve

Nick saw the engagement ring on her finger and the bloodlust rose in him like bile. He had to end this, and damn soon.

With the implosion only days away, his work with the demolition company was becoming more pressing. So pressing, Todd had assigned one of the newer guys, Bill Hodges, to watch Jenny for longer and longer stretches. Nick wasn't thrilled with the arrangement, but there wasn't much he could do about it. Since that day they'd made love, he'd only been with her a few hours here and there, mostly in the afternoons, when she was with Patrick.

They hadn't had a chance to talk, although she'd effectively communicated her desperation in a hundred ways.

She was getting panicky, and he couldn't blame her. Marriage to Todd was the ultimate nightmare. His worry was that she'd do something foolish, which would alert Todd to her intention to escape.

Perhaps Todd already knew she was up to something. That could explain why he'd sent her to her room each night, directly after dinner.

In their brief snatches of conversation, she'd told Nick that Todd was more and more preoccupied. He was even more secretive than usual, but he had told her to prepare for an extended trip after the Fourth. A honeymoon that would take them to Europe and Asia. Which meant that Nick was right—whatever he was planning was going to happen on the Fourth.

The demolition team had performed many implosions of even larger magnitude than the El Rio, but given the number of tourists who would come out for the show, they were being extraordinarily careful in the planning stages. They kept Nick informed each step of the way.

Nick, in turn, worked with the local authorities to ensure nothing would go wrong. A very tight area was going to be cordoned off to the public. One of the conditions was that the building implode in its own footprint, with no margin for error. All the tests had gone well, but still, it would require massive crowd-control personnel, which worked well, as Nick made sure most of the temporary hires were agents. Todd, whatever he was planning, would be surrounded.

Nick felt certain they didn't have to worry about the bomb being detonated on the Fourth. Todd wasn't suicidal. He also felt sure the ultimate target wasn't going to be Las Vegas or anywhere on the West Coast. Alerts had been given to all agencies, and there was heightened surveillance at all points of entry. Nick was fairly sure all the players were already in town, but no one aside from the Pakistani had been pinpointed.

For today, at least, his work on the implosion was done so he could spend some time with Jenny. He wanted to find a safe zone, so he could find out what she was up to.

He knocked on her door and she opened it within a few seconds. Her smile seemed forced, which wasn't anything unusual. The engagement, if one could call it that, had surpassed her limits. Did Todd not see that? Or did he simply not care? Probably the latter.

"How are things at the El Rio going?" she asked, as if she gave a damn.

"Great. It should go off without a hitch. Listen, I was thinking this afternoon it might be nice to take Patrick to the pool."

Her mouth opened as her eyes filled with dread, but before she could protest he said, "I mean, the private pool outside your suite. Just the three of us."

Jenny relaxed. He'd known, before he asked, that there was no way she'd go out in public in a bikini, not the kind Todd insisted she wear. But she might go for the private pool. If he could get her in the water, they could speak. Todd was good, but he wasn't a magician. There were no microphones in the deep end. There had been a directional mike off the patio door, but that was, as of an hour ago, dysfunctional.

"Sure, that sounds like fun," she said. "I'll go change."

"Great. I'll go tell Mrs. Norris, so she can get Patrick ready."

With a smile that looked nearly real, Jenny headed off, but before he reached the door, she stopped him. "Please ask Mrs. Norris to put Patrick in a T-shirt and trunks. I don't want to risk him getting burned."

"You got it."

She smiled again, a little brighter this time, and went off to change. The thought of her in the closet was something he couldn't afford to contemplate, so he went next door. Mrs. Norris was as pleasant as always, getting Patrick ready per instructions with a minimum of fuss.

Just as they were heading out of Patrick's bedroom, Jenny knocked. She wore a sleeveless, floor-length dress to cover her suit and a wide-brimmed hat for her head. He'd never seen anything so pretty.

"Here's his sunscreen," Mrs. Norris said, handing a tube to Jenny. "He's eaten lunch, but I sliced a few carrots for a snack. That and some juice should see him through."

"Thank you."

"If you need anything, I'm right here."

"We'll be fine. You should take a little time for yourself. Relax. Get out for a bit."

"I may do just that." She kissed Patrick, who was wiggling ferociously in Nick's arms. "Be good, lovie."

"Swimming!"

"Right on, my man," Nick said. "To the pool."

"To the pool!" Patrick repeated, although about five decibels louder.

It didn't take long to get to the deck outside Todd's

suite. It was, as everything else that belonged to the man, opulent and extravagant in the extreme.

The pool itself was shaped like a slot machine, complete with a lap-pool arm. The entire deck surface was marble tile, and each of the slot's windows had the company logo in bright red letters. At the deep end, there was a diving board and a slide.

A separate whirlpool, raised on a platform, was nearer the outdoor cabana. It looked to Nick as though it could hold a dozen people, easily. Then there were the overstuffed lounge chairs, tables with bright, logo umbrellas, and a complete bar. There was also a barbecue range to the right of the bar. It was ideal for entertaining, although Nick knew Todd didn't care for the water.

Jenny got settled on a lounger while Patrick jumped up and down in his anxiety to get in the water. Bowing to the inevitable, she slathered every available surface with sunscreen, then pushed small inflatable rings onto his upper arms. By the time she was finished, he was in a frenzy.

Nick stripped down to his trunks. "I'll take him," he said. "You take your time."

"You do know how to swim, right?"

He nodded. "I do. I even got my life-saving badge from the Red Cross. He'll be fine."

"Thank you." She handed the boy over, their fingers brushing during the exchange. It wasn't much, but it was the most contact they'd had in a couple of days. Nick reacted in a most masculine fashion and hoped the water was cold.

It wasn't. It was quite warm, although not uncomfortable. Patrick started splashing immediately, so Nick dove under, just to get wet.

For the next half hour, the two of them played. Patrick loved being tossed into the water from Nick's shoulder. The first time, he'd come up sputtering, but after that, he just held his nose and closed his mouth. It was a hell of a workout for Nick, lifting and tossing him over and over.

Finally he cried uncle and sequestered Patrick in the shallow end of the pool, on the steps.

Nick looked over to see Jenny, her hat and dress still on, sunglasses shading her eyes, a book in her hands. "Hey, you. Get on in here."

She shook her head. "You're doing fine."

"Come on, Jenny. Don't make me come up there."

"Don't you dare."

"I do dare, so you'd better get your behind in gear."

She shook her head again, but then he gave her what he hoped was a clear signal, lifting his brow. It worked. She stood, took her dress off.

Nick swallowed as he got a load of her in one of the tiniest bikinis he'd ever seen. She was barely covered. Clearly, it was a Todd purchase, because Jenny was far too modest to have picked it out herself.

She took off her hat and sunglasses, and did a quick swipe of her upper body with sunscreen.

Nick turned his attention to Patrick. It was much safer that way.

Jenny finished with the sunscreen and looked around for something that would delay her entry into the pool.

She'd run out of props. She would play with Patrick, which would be good. It would make her smile seem natural and, maybe, if she were lucky, she'd actually forget for a moment the joke that was her life.

She went to the shallow end of the pool where marble coins flowed out of the oversize bin, and stepped in, pleasantly surprised at the temperature. It made sense. There hadn't been a day in the past month that was under a hundred degrees.

She wasn't outside enough to be bothered by it, and it kind of felt good after the steady cool temperature of her cell.

Patrick caught sight of her and went nuts, waving his arms like little propellers. He looked so adorable she couldn't help but laugh. My God, he was so precious. She couldn't stand her separations from him. The idea of sending him away to military school made her physically ill. That Todd could even think of taking a child so young to a building implosion was insane. The noise alone was going to give Patrick nightmares for weeks, if not months. He already had such an active imagination, sometimes he frightened her.

Mostly, though, he filled her with such peace that nothing, save his safety, could shake her.

She was plenty shaken now.

"Mommy, watch me."

"Okay, honey."

Patrick stood on the second step, where the water came up to the middle of his thigh. He spread his arms out wide, balancing the inflatable rings, then, with a mighty grunt, jumped off the step to land on the first step with a splash.

Jenny applauded wildly. A glance to her right showed her that Nick was clapping, too. Patrick beamed, eating up the attention as if he were starved for it.

It wasn't true, of course. She saw him every day and she couldn't have wished for a better nanny. But it felt true.

"He's something else, isn't he?"

She hadn't heard Nick move in beside her. "Yes, he is."

"It must have been hard, doing it all by yourself. Hiding."

"Not as hard as this."

"I know." He looked behind him, then at Patrick who was doing his jump for the third time. After the splash, Nick clapped, then turned back to Jenny. "Come deeper. As far out as you can."

She nodded, although the idea of talking in Todd's own pool made her very nervous. Ever since the night at the restaurant, she'd been as paranoid as a jewel thief in Tiffany's. She had tried to get more information, something concrete that would ensure her safety and Todd's conviction, but he'd either stuck too close to her or sent her to her room.

Maybe he knew she'd been spying, but if that were the case, why would he want to marry her? Whatever the reason, escape wasn't looking good.

She walked to the edge of the shallow section of the pool, the resistance of the water tugging at her as if in warning. She used to love to swim. She'd even been on the swim team in high school. In this obscene bathing suit, she'd never go to a public pool again. It was humiliating. She felt naked.

Nick had scooped Patrick up and had him riding on his shoulders. They'd reached the deep end already and Nick swam around, Patrick splashing and kicking the whole way. He wasn't exactly being a delicate swan about it, either. Nick would have bruises come tomorrow.

They paddled her way and stopped, Patrick firmly held by Nick's sturdy hands.

"You need to tell me what you're doing," he said.

"I'm not doing anything."

"I'm serious, Jen. Tell me. It's all coming down—and I mean soon—and we can't afford to blow it."

"I'm not kidding. I haven't done anything. He's watching me like a hawk. Either that, or I'm in my room. That's it."

"Yeah, he's been keeping me away, too."

"You think he knows?"

"No. If he did, we'd be dead. But he might suspect. I personally think that whatever he's got going is right around the corner."

"Well?"

He shook his head. "I think he's going to be doing something serious on the Fourth of July."

"What does that mean?"

"I'm not sure, but it's going to shake things up, and not in a good way. I think we're talking heavy money, foreign investors, more than likely highly illegal."

"Oh, my."

"Yeah."

"Do you know who's involved?"

"No. But we're going to find out. That's why we have to be so careful. Jenny, all I can tell you is the stakes are big, and if he stands to win, he also stands to lose. Todd losing isn't something you need to see."

She studied his face, searching for a clue. He was still an enigma to her. "What's your role in this?"

"I'm going to make sure I win. And that you don't get hurt."

"What does that mean? Damn it, aren't you ever going to tell me the truth?"

He opened his mouth, but his words were cut short as the patio door hissed open. She whirled around to see Todd standing just outside the door.

"Hi, Todd," she said, a little too sprightly. "Want to come swimming with us?"

He stared at her for a long time. Then shook his head. "No. I've got a meeting coming up in a few minutes. But I will sit down and watch for a while."

"Sure I can't convince you to take a small dip? The water feels wonderful."

"No, you go on ahead. Pretend I'm not here. Go on."

She smiled brightly, then held out her arms. Nick picked up the cue seamlessly and backed up. When he was about five feet away, he lifted Patrick by the boy's armpits and stood the toddler on his knee. Then, after a count of three, he launched Patrick into the air, right smack into her waiting arms.

Patrick squealed with delight and when Jenny looked

at the deck, Todd was smiling happily. Weren't they just one big happy family?

She focused totally on Patrick, hardly looking at Nick, afraid that she'd give herself away. Wishing for once he'd come clean. If she only understood what he wanted…what he hoped to gain, then she could help him. Or forget him.

She kept a check on Todd as she and Patrick played. It was at least a hundred and five, yet Todd looked cool and comfortable, as if sweat didn't dare mess up his suit. She knew that one. He'd gone to Italy to have it tailored from material he'd had specially designed. There was only one suit like it in the world. The tie, pale gray, like the suit, was made from silkworms in China. Todd owned the factory. His shoes were also Italian, made of the finest leather by a craftsman who was technically retired but still worked for his best and only customer.

Nick was right. She didn't want to be around when Todd lost. The only thing that she'd ever seen him lose was her. And she knew how that had turned out.

Sweet was also right. She was expendable. But looking at Todd as he watched her son gave her goose bumps. If he ever knew…

"Jenny."

She smiled. "Yes?"

"Why don't you let Nick take Patrick to Mrs. Norris. We're going to be out late tonight. You might like to rest."

"No, I'm fine, Todd."

"Jenny."

She nodded. Turned to Patrick, who was trying to catch the water in his little fists. "Honey, kiss me good-bye. Mommy has to go in. Nick will take you back to Mrs. Norris."

He kissed her, then went back to his game. No crying, no histrionics. It hadn't even been a month and already Mrs. Norris was a suitable replacement for her.

It wasn't fair. And it wasn't right. And she'd better go in and rest before Todd used her delay as a reason to make her even more miserable. She climbed out of the pool, Todd's gaze making her want to cover herself. She felt his eyes on her back as she went for her towel. Did he take pleasure in her humiliation? Of course he did. That's why he dressed her this way. To own her.

She wrapped herself in her towel and gathered her things. Then she went to Todd, kissed him on the cheek. As she turned to leave, he grabbed her wrist. Hard.

"Take off the towel," he said.

She knew better than to argue. She let the towel fall to her feet.

He looked her over as if she were a piece of beef. And then, to her horror, he reached up, grabbed her bikini top and pulled it off. She covered her bare breasts with her hands, turned so Patrick wouldn't see.

Todd laughed. Slapped her on the rear. "Run along. Get some sleep. I want you in a party mood tonight."

She left the towel, afraid to pick it up, and ran into his suite. Mortification burned her face as she made her way through to his front door. Everything was made just perfect when she ran into Sweet.

His laughter followed her all the way down the hall.

NICK ADDED that little demonstration of abuse to the list of why he was going to kill Todd and smile while doing it. The son of a bitch. He'd done that just to humiliate her. In front of her son, no less.

But he didn't let it show. He just gathered Patrick up in his arms and headed for the pool steps.

"I don't wanna!"

"I know, but it's time."

"Don't!"

"Patrick, this isn't negotiable. You're going in."

"I hate you."

"I'm sure you do, kiddo, but trust me, you'll get over it."

"I won't."

"Yeah. You will." He lifted the boy up to eye level. "I'm a lovable guy. You won't be able to help yourself."

Patrick burst into tears. Not the response he was going for. It didn't matter. He wanted the kid away from Todd. Far away. And the best thing he could do now was to keep it light.

He got Patrick on land, took off the arm inflatables, then dried him briskly with his towel. It didn't take long, Patrick crying the whole time. Finally he slipped off his trunks, dried off, and pulled on his own slacks. He'd deal with his shirt later, after his shower.

Todd was still sitting there, watching the whole play as if he were the director. He didn't say anything as Nick picked Patrick up, gathered the last of their stuff and headed for the door. And then he didn't say goodbye to Patrick, or mention anything to Nick about work. He made some off-the-wall comment about Nick's birthmark. Weird.

Chapter Thirteen

"Welcome to Las Vegas, Mr. Petrov."

"Thank you, Inspector. It's nice to be somewhere warm."

Edward Potereiko was at the U.S. Customs Office in Las Vegas. He smiled warmly despite his nervousness. His years of military service served him well, allowing him to present a casual demeanor at the final point of danger on his long journey; if they discovered what was in the aluminum case amid the junk furniture he'd bought in Kushiro, the game was most definitely over.

"Well, it's a dry heat, Mr. Petrov. Most people find it less bothersome than if it's muggy."

"I do not think I will ever get used to this level of air-conditioning."

"It's different if you have to work in the heat all day, believe me."

"I am sure it is, Inspector."

The man finished going through Potereiko's paperwork and opened a drawer, withdrawing a handful of rubber stamps. He began imprinting the various documents. "You realize we still have to take a look inside that crate, sir."

"Of course. Although in Long Beach, they told me it was a formality." They'd also stamped the documents in Long Beach. Bureaucracies were the same the world over.

"So, it's all personal items totaling less than two thousand dollars?"

"Yes, sir."

"And where will you be taking it from here?"

Potereiko pulled a slip of paper from his pocket and peered at it before handing it across the counter. "I will have somebody pick it up as soon as it passes inspection. I have rented a small house."

The contrast between the two men could not have been more marked. Even in a Moscow-tailored suit with the tie loosened, Edward Potereiko's demeanor bore the mark of decades of undiluted military precision, while the inspector, although in uniform, appeared somehow unkempt. The former colonel resisted the temptation to point out a button whose threads were giving way.

The inspector noted the address, a lower-rent area in the northeast area of Las Vegas. "You'll be living on Cincinnati?"

"If I were not staying for some time, I would not need any personal items."

The inspector looked over Potereiko's passport—in the name of Ivan Petrov of course—and noted several earlier visas to the United States. "I see you've been here before, Mr. Petrov."

"It is always a pleasure to visit the cradle of liberty."

The inspector smiled and Potereiko was reminded of how gullible Americans were. Always easily distracted with the vaguest of compliments. So insecure about their country and its place in the world. And yet so arrogant.

"What's the purpose of your visit?"

Potereiko began to feel a twinge of irritation. He'd been through all this with Immigration, and didn't feel the need to explain himself to every petty bureaucrat. Still, he didn't want that crate to be inspected too carefully. He forced another smile. "I am consulting with Todd Industries on a project. A liaison with the Soviet government."

The other man whistled as his eyes widened. "Wow, Todd. Doesn't get much bigger than that."

"That is my understanding."

The shorter man handed Potereiko's papers back to him, taking one last look at the shipping manifest. "Well, it's getting late in the day, but we'll get over to Tiger Shipping at nine in the morning and try to get that cleared for you."

"I would be deeply grateful. Thank you, Inspector." Edward thrust his hand forward and the surprised Customs official shook it. Potereiko resisted the temptation to squeeze until the man dropped to his knees. "I will see you in the morning, then."

"Well, somebody will be there." The inspector returned to shuffling papers behind the counter as Potereiko headed for the door.

A wall of heat hit him and he paused for a moment,

letting the warmth and the airport bustle wash over him. On the other side of the building he could hear the familiar whine of jets, and to the east the sound of a— what did the Americans call it?—a freeway, so much busier than the liveliest Russian highway, even Moscow at lunchtime. His cab was still waiting in front of the Customs office.

He strode to the vehicle and paused to give the driver time to open the door for him, but the man didn't budge and Potereiko sighed as he climbed into the back seat.

"Gonna have to charge you for the wait, ya know?" the driver said around a wad of gum.

"Of course. I need to go to this address now, please. We'll only be there for a few minutes." Potereiko leaned forward and handed the tattered piece of paper with the Cincinnati address to the driver.

The man glanced at it, nodded, handed it back and shifted into gear.

Potereiko rolled his window down, ignoring the driver's glare in the mirror. Edward enjoyed the warm air blowing on his face.

The car worked its way across downtown toward the northeast. Potereiko marveled that the casino lights were on even though the sun showed little sign of disappearing. About fifteen minutes later the cab pulled up in front of a small one-story house.

"This's it," the driver said.

"Would you mind waiting for a few minutes?"

The cabbie looked dubious. "Look, man. I picked

you up at the airport, I waited at Customs, I brought you here. For all I know, you ain't got a dime."

Potereiko pulled out a silver money clip with a red-enameled star on it. He slipped a fifty-dollar bill out and handed it to the driver. "Let me know when this is not enough," he said.

"You got it, buddy," the man said, quickly stuffing the bill into his pocket.

Basking in the warmth, Potereiko strolled to the front door of the small dwelling. A small box with a combination lock hung on the door latch and Potereiko pulled another slip of paper from his pocket, noted the numbers, then bent to the lock box. When it opened, he removed the key and used it to open the door.

It swung open with a bang and he stepped into the vacant living room.

It was perfect.

He wandered around, looking at the other rooms; the small bedroom, the bathroom, the miniscule kitchen. Everywhere, his footsteps echoed from the walls, and the musty smell of emptiness tickled his nostrils. He stepped once more into the front room and stood looking around, smiling.

Although barely larger than a Moscow luxury apartment, the house only had to be big enough for the crate to be carried in. Once inside, he would open it and remove the only thing of value and take it with him. Then, in a very short time, with twenty-five million American dollars in cash, the man who had entered the country as Ivan Petrov would disappear, leaving the mystery of the empty crate in the empty house to those who worried about such things.

That is, if the Customs inspection went well.

And if he could survive C. Randall Todd.

All the former colonel's senses told him to be wary of the man, and he'd taken every precaution. Todd would not know where the bomb was until the moment Potereiko had the money. And the exchange would take place publicly. By the same token, he had refused the offer of a luxury suite at the Xanadu. A savage place, indeed, he thought, remembering Coleridge.

Perhaps he'd retire to the Bahamas, Edward thought. Certainly somewhere with kinder winters than either Russia or the Ukraine. With that amount of money, getting it out of the United States would be his only problem.

He walked out, carefully locked the door and walked down the sidewalk to the cab, pausing to look back once again.

"Thank you, driver," he said, opening the rear door. "To the Algiers, please."

JENNY CHECKED the bedside clock. It was five minutes to three, time for her to go.

Todd slept soundly beside her, his arm cradling his head, his white hair vivid against the navy blue sheets even in the dark of his bedroom.

If he woke up, it shouldn't alarm him that she'd gone. It probably would have surprised him more to find her here. The night had been a long one, dinner at a fund-raising benefit for breast cancer research, with dancing afterward. Todd was his charming self, busy chatting it up with the influential of Vegas society, while she mostly stood silent by his side, showing off her ring by putting her left hand on his arm. Of course, he hadn't been gauche enough to announce the value of the ring, but the word had mysteriously spread nonetheless. By the end of the evening, her jaw had ached from her forced happiness.

They'd come back to the room just after two and she'd fully expected another trip to hell, but nothing had happened. He'd simply told her to get into bed and he'd gone to sleep next to her. No words, no recriminations. In its own way, this scared her more than anything he could have done.

She hadn't had room to be too distraught. She was too busy being preoccupied by the events about to take place.

When she'd gone to her room for her nap this afternoon, she'd stopped by Mrs. Norris's room. Taking her life in her hands, she'd asked the nanny to do her a favor. To slip a note to Nick. If all had gone well, she would see him at her door in a few minutes. She planned to take him through her suite in the dark, all the way back to the closet. Her safe space. There, she intended to break her silence and tell him the truth about Patrick.

If, in fact, all hell was about to break loose, she wanted him to know. She hoped it was the right thing to do. Seeing him with Patrick this afternoon had made it clear that she couldn't continue the pretense. Nick had a right to know he was a father. Maybe, if miracles occurred and they all lived through this, they could actually be parents to the boy. Whether they would ever be a couple, she had no idea. It seemed too much to hope for.

One thing for sure, she couldn't be with him if he continued to work for Xanadu. Even with Todd gone, she wouldn't be able to stand it. Once this was over, she never wanted to see Las Vegas again. She'd probably be in the Witness Security Program, anyway, so it was foolish to entertain thoughts of happily-ever-after, but she couldn't help it. She had to have some dreams left, even if they were completely unrealistic.

She slipped out of the bed and, moving as quietly as she knew how, got her robe from inside the bathroom. After she slipped it on, she crept through the suite. It was dark and quiet, but she made it unscathed. The door was a little trickier, but she had memorized the alarm combination and a few moments later was in the hallway. She knew there were cameras here, but her presence shouldn't make any waves. She trusted that Nick would find some safe way of getting to her room.

When she was just a few feet from her door, the lights in the hallway went out. After her heart stopped pounding and she remembered how to breathe again, she realized that was Nick's solution.

She walked the few remaining steps and when she pulled her key card out of her robe pocket, saw his shadow approach.

It was so dark, she couldn't make out any of his features. In fact, she wouldn't have known who it was, if she hadn't memorized his scent. It was Nick, all right, and it was his hand on the small of her back as she opened the door.

In complete silence, not even a footfall to be heard, they walked through her suite until they reached her bedroom. The darkness here was almost complete, so he found her hand, put it on his shoulder and led the way, inching past the armoire, the chaise and the bed until he found the closet.

Once inside, she exhaled, although her heart still raced. It was terrifying, and she hated it. She felt as though she'd spent half her life hiding, running, being scared. To be carefree, feel the kind of safety most of the world took for granted, that was her dream. To not worry about her son being corrupted, or being kidnapped…was that so much to ask?

"Close your eyes," Nick said. "I'm going to turn on a light."

She obeyed, and even though she could tell it wasn't the overhead light, the brightness still made her wince, the contrast from the dark was so intense. A few moments later her eyes adjusted and she opened them. Nick was right in front of her, studying her face, not touching her, but oh, so close.

They each leaned forward until their lips met. She melted against him and his arms came around her back, and there was nothing but safety in that hold. Only comfort.

"Jenny," he whispered. "Oh, my God. You shouldn't have risked it. Don't you understand? It's so close, and there's so much to lose."

"I had to. It's you who doesn't understand. I have something to tell you."

He kissed her again, deeply, sharing breath, sharing hope. He pulled her tightly against him, the thin robe letting her feel his strength. For the moment there was no Todd, no engagement, nothing but the two of them coming together. It was impossible to be still and they moved their lips, tongues, hands, as each of them did their best to lose themselves in the other. When he pulled back, she gasped in much-needed air, but there was no way she was finished.

He moaned as he touched her breast, cupping her, then gently squeezing. His gaze locked on hers once more, pleaded with his eyes.

She understood. For all they knew, this was the last time, the only time, they'd be this close. She wanted nothing more than to take off her robe, to lie down on the soft cushions and open herself to him. She wanted him inside her, she wanted…

Instead she pushed him back. There were more important things to worry about now. She'd denied herself for so long, she knew she wouldn't die, even though it felt beyond her endurance.

Nick's hand left her and curled into a fist. "Okay. We'll talk. I have something to tell you, too. I've made arrangements for someone to get you and Patrick. I don't know exactly how, or who, but you've got to be ready. You won't have time to take anything except the clothes on your back, but don't worry about it. You'll be safe and taken care of. If I were you, I'd be sure I was wearing that ring and any other jewelry you can get away with. It'll help later on."

"What do you mean, you've made arrangements?"

"Just listen, damn it. Do what they tell you. Don't argue. They'll take you to safety."

"Who? What are you talking about?"

He closed his eyes, then slowly opened them again. "I'm with the FBI."

She nodded as pieces of the puzzle fell neatly into place. "Thank God. I hoped. But hoping hasn't gotten me very far lately."

"You can stop hoping and start counting your blessings. Two more days. That's it. You'll be out of here."

Tears came to her eyes and her body, for some weird reason, started to shake. He was an FBI agent. A good guy. Trying to take down Todd. The whole time… "Why didn't you tell me?"

"I couldn't compromise the mission. But more important, I couldn't compromise you. If you slipped…"

"I'm not in the habit of slipping."

"I know. But he couldn't force you to say something you didn't know."

"Fair enough. But tell me something. Why were you so ugly when I came back? So mean?"

He looked away, suddenly finding a great interest in her Fendi bag. "I thought if you hated me, you'd make Todd replace me as your bodyguard."

"Not that he would have listened, but why would you want that?"

He turned on her. "You don't know?"

"What?"

"Good God, woman. Can't you see what you do to me? When I'm around you, I lose all sense of proportion. I don't give a damn about saving the world, just you." He laughed. "I couldn't do anything right. That first time I had you in here, when we could finally talk, all I'd intended to do was to scare the hell out of you. Make certain you never wanted to speak to me again. You know how that ended."

"Really?"

"Yes, really." He moved closer to her again, ran the back of his hand down her cheek. "You mess me up. Always have. I didn't worry about Sweet or any of Todd's other goons. You were the one who was going to get me killed."

"I don't want you killed."

He grinned. "I'm glad to hear it."

"I'm not joking, Nick. When this is over, I'd really like to…you know, figure this out."

"Go on."

She met his gaze and the words became unimportant. Because she saw he knew just exactly what she meant. "Well, for one thing, I'd like to talk to you in a normal tone of voice."

"Hmm."

"And I'd like to hold hands in public."

"You wild woman."

"There's more."

"Oh?"

She nodded slowly. "I'd like to make love in a bed. And be as noisy as I want."

"You? Noisy?"

"You have no idea."

"My, my."

"There's a lot you don't know about me, Nick Mason."

His smile got a little crooked as his eyes softened. "There's so much I do know. You're the strongest woman I've ever met. You're incredibly resourceful. Braver than I could hope to be on my best day. Through all the hell, you've kept your humanity. Your gentleness. There isn't anyone else I'd want at my side."

That did it. She just fell apart. Tears flowed, her nose ran; he had to hold her up. It didn't stop all that quickly, either. The more he petted her hair, the more he whispered, "Shh," the more she blubbered. Finally, finally, the tears slowed to a trickle and she was able to stand.

"Here."

She looked down to see that he'd grabbed a scarf. It was a Hermès, worth about five hundred dollars. She took it and blew her nose as hard as she could. When she was through, she tossed it into the back of the closet and turned to him. "I'm better now."

"Good, because we've got to go."

"No."

"It would be a real damn shame if we screwed up now."

"There's not even time for kissing?"

He shook his head. Right up until he grabbed her by the shoulders and kissed her.

Chapter Fourteen

Sweet woke to the sound of his cell phone ringing. He shoved at the woman half-draped over him and grabbed it from the nightstand. The clock, its green glow the only light in the room, read 4:50. "Sweet."

"Henry, I need you to do something for me."

"Yes, sir."

"It's going to require a bit of acting, but not much. And, don't fret, I think you'll enjoy the task."

Sweet sat up. Rubbed his eyes. He wished he could spit out the taste of stale booze and cigars, but that could wait. "What is it?"

"I need to get a sample of Nick Mason's blood."

Sweet grinned. "Hell, I'll give you six quarts, if you like."

Todd laughed. "That won't be necessary. Yet. I don't want him to suspect a thing. I don't need much blood, just enough to get his type. And I'd like it by midmorning. Do you think you can handle that?"

"With pleasure."

"I thought so. If my hunch is correct, which it most

likely is, you're going to enjoy the next phase even more."

"I'm sure I will."

"Remember, I don't want him suspicious. And I don't require much blood. Do this well, Henry. You know what's at stake."

"I do, sir."

Todd hung up and Sweet disconnected. He took a swig of the now-warm beer sitting behind his clock. He wouldn't be going back to sleep. Not for a while, at least.

"Sweetie?"

He turned to the woman curled up in his bed. She was a dancer from Cheetah's, the nudie bar off Western. A beauty, too. Tall, blond, slender. Real classy. On their way to the elevator, one of the doormen had mistaken her for Jenny. Right. That cold bitch wouldn't be in his bed. He liked his women friendly.

"Don't go back to sleep," he said, throwing his covers aside. He got up, naked, and walked to his bathroom. He was hard again and it wasn't just because of what's-her-name.

Todd had finally come to his senses about Mason. Of all the jobs he could do for the boss, the one he'd most like would be to take that bastard down. He wanted to hurt him, bad. Make him beg. Make him want to die.

But he'd be smart. Get the blood real unobtrusive-like. Smart. And when the time was right, he'd give the boss a show he'd never forget.

NICK CURLED HIS BODY around Jenny's as he caught his breath. He was an idiot to have pressed his luck like this, but he wasn't strong enough to walk away from the invitation in her eyes. Jenny scrunched in closer, rubbing her backside against him and, amazingly, he stirred again. He'd figured he was down for the count, but he hadn't reckoned with Jenny's effect on him. He thought about her little wish list. Talking normally, about anything they wished. Holding hands. Her crying out as she came to a shuddering climax.

They were good wishes, and he intended to make them come true. If he found her. Which wasn't going to be easy.

Owen had some of the top tactical minds in the FBI working around the clock to set up a massive sting on Todd and his empire. Nick had finally convinced the powers that be, damn powerful powers, that the best way to handle the situation was to leave Todd alone until the Fourth, then to strike on every level.

Owen was going to take over Xanadu and close down Todd's operations. The FBI were also going to take over all Todd's other properties. There would be special agents posted at every block for five miles around the El Rio, with complete teams and safe cars at strategic areas ready to swoop in on Todd the moment he made his move to get the weapon, but not before. Because if they moved too soon, whoever the hell was selling would simply walk away and sell to someone else. That couldn't happen.

Nick himself was going to stick to Todd like glue and make sure the man went down if he tried anything funny. Meanwhile, Jenny and Patrick would be swept away, taken to a safe house where they'd wait till it was all over and Todd was behind bars, and then they'd be given asylum in witness security. Unless, of course, Nick got his wish and Todd didn't live to see the fire-works at midnight.

Jenny would still be sequestered, but it wouldn't be quite so permanent. Just until the debriefings were over. Then she'd be free to go wherever she chose. She'd be free, for the first time since she'd met C. Randall.

Nick's future was a little less certain. All he knew for sure was that he wouldn't work undercover and he wouldn't work in Las Vegas. The rest was up for grabs.

"Nick?"

"Yeah, babe."

"Remember I said before that I had something to tell you?"

"Sure." He whispered the word into her ear and then was completely unable to resist nibbling on her perfect lobe.

She wriggled away, turned on the cushion so they faced each other. There wasn't enough contact for his taste, so he pulled her closer, wrapped his arm and his leg over her side. Better.

"Are you done?"

"For the moment."

"Okay, because this is important."

He heard a slight quiver in her voice and he stopped fidgeting. "I'm all yours."

She took a big breath and let it out slowly. The warmth of her breath hit him on the chin. It made him aware of the temperature, which was a little chilly. "Hold it," he said, untangling himself long enough to find her robe and pull it over her body. Once he saw she was good, he got back in position. "Okay. Now."

"Is there anything else? Do you want to straighten up? Maybe try on a few clothes?"

"Nope. I'm good."

She laughed softly. It wasn't really her laugh at all. While he'd never heard her cry out when she was making love, he had heard her laugh. Big-time. She had one of those laughs that make everyone else crack up, even if they hadn't heard the joke. Hell, she made complete strangers break up just by hearing her let go. She hadn't laughed like that in too long.

"Look at me."

He focused, curious now.

"First, know that I had good reason for not telling you this before. I'm sorry, but I did."

"Okay."

"Patrick," she said. Then she kind of swallowed. Oddly her eyes filled up with tears.

And he knew. "He's mine, isn't he?"

She blinked, releasing one tear. "Yes."

Nick rolled over onto his back. Patrick was his son. His kid. Not Todd's.

No wonder he'd liked the boy so much. Damn, he was a bright kid. On the ball. Good-looking, too. He'd be a heartbreaker, that's for sure. Just like his dad.

Holy… He was a father. He had a child with Jenny, who meant more to him than any woman, any person, ever had. He hadn't planned on being a dad, but man, he'd sure picked the right mom to do it with.

He rolled back onto his side and found Jenny staring at him with wide, frightened eyes. He touched her cheek, lifted a tear with his index finger. "We have a kid," he whispered. "How do you like that?"

"I like it fine. How about you?"

He grinned. "Well, if you want to know the truth…"

She punched him in the arm. Hard. "Nick."

"I'm knocked out," he said. "No kidding. Patrick's an amazing kid. And you. You're…"

"I'm what?"

"You're the one I'm in love with."

"Oh, God."

"And on that sentimental, sweet note, we have to get the hell out of here before we're caught."

"Right," she said. "Exactly."

Then she kissed him.

He kissed her back. It didn't feel any different. Fatherhood wasn't half-bad.

SWEET HAD DONE his homework. He didn't need much blood, it just had to be as clean as possible. He'd thought about just beating it out of the guy, but Todd had said that that would have to wait. But the fight angle still appealed. If he couldn't whack Nick, he could do the next best thing: watch.

"Uh, Mr. Sweet? Nick Mason's kind of a big guy. Won't he, uh, clean my clock?"

Sweet leaned back in his office chair. "You don't

have to go five rounds with him. Just hit him once, in the face. Make him bleed. That's it."

Frank Yoder, one of the security guys over at Le Mystique, looked as though was going to be sick. "Yeah, but after that, he's gonna kill me."

"No, he won't. I'll be there to stop him." Yoder wasn't thrilled and Sweet knew he'd like nothing better than to walk out the door and keep on walking till he hit Arizona. But the man had taken some serious markers out at the hotel casino and there wasn't a chance in hell he could pay them back in a year. He was already having most of his wages garnished. "This will wipe your slate clean, Frank. No debt. You keep your hard-earned cash. All for hitting some guy you don't even know."

Yoder chewed on his lower lip for another minute, then nodded. "Yeah, sure. It's a great deal, Mr. Sweet. You just tell me what to do and I'm your man."

Sweet sat straight. He wondered if he should tell Yoder he wasn't being asked, he was being told. Had he refused the job, he'd have found himself in the middle of the beautiful Mojave communing with nature. With both kneecaps broken. "Wise decision, Frank. I want you at the Mongol bar at Xanadu at four this afternoon. I want you to smell like you're drunk. Now, I don't care if you're drunk or not, but you're going to act like you are. You're going to be real convincing. So convincing, there won't be any questions later."

"Drunk. Got it."

"Good. I'm going to come into the bar along with Nick Mason. You're going to come up to us. And with no warning whatsoever, you're going to smash Nick's face in. One punch, to the mouth or nose. Preferably the nose. Then two of my men are going to get you out of there. You won't go easily. Remember, you're drunk. Very drunk."

"Yeah, yeah. Drunk."

"You'll be taken to a car and driven to your home. If you've done your job as described, your markers will be torn up. If you don't... Well, let's just say you wouldn't want to find out."

Yoder took in a deep breath and let it out slow. "I understand."

"Good. See you at three."

"Yes, sir. Three."

Sweet swiveled his chair and looked out the window as he listened to his man walk to the door then leave. He loved his job. The best thing he'd ever done was hook up with Todd.

He thought about that a lot. How Todd had saved his life all those years ago. Taken him under his wing. Taught him how to dress, how to be strong, how to make everyone listen to what he had to say. Todd had given him a life he'd never have imagined. Hell, he was a rich man, and he'd only get richer.

He'd wondered what Todd needed with Nick's blood, but he'd let the thought go. That's one of the most important lessons he'd learned. When it came to carrying out Todd's orders, he didn't ask questions. He didn't think, he just performed. It worked out well for both of them.

The only thing Sweet didn't like about his job was

that bastard Nick Mason. What did the boss see in that guy, anyway? He was always with the questions, always second-guessing Todd. And Todd didn't seem to mind, which Sweet didn't understand at all. But Todd had said to let it be. So Sweet had.

Now it looked as though Todd had seen the light. Whatever Nick had done, he'd pissed the boss off, and that was just fine. Probably tried to get into Jenny's pants, which was like the stupidest thing anyone could do. Didn't Mason get it? Jenny was Todd's *property*. Mason might as well try to steal Xanadu from under Todd's nose.

Sweet knew just how he wanted to kill Mason. He'd thought about it a lot. Discarded a whole bunch of plans as too easy. Not painful enough. He had it now, though. It would take almost a full day. Yeah. Watch the man squirm like a worm on a hook. It was gonna be great.

JENNY FINISHED APPLYING her lip gloss, checked herself in the mirror one last time, then headed out. She was having lunch with Todd. They were going to discuss the wedding. It was ludicrous. They never discussed anything. Todd simply told her what was going to happen and that was that. The difference here was that she knew the wedding wasn't going to take place. All she had to do was not give herself away. It would be tempting to sit back and relax, to let the whole thing pass in a blur. But then Todd would know something was up. She had to act as if she really did think the wedding was going to happen and that she hated the idea, but was pretending not to hate the idea. Too complicated. Too many ways it could go wrong.

She also had to avoid thinking about Nick. Nothing would broadcast trouble to Todd more than the goofy grin that was just aching to come out. Nick loved her. Nick loved that they had Patrick. Nick was a good guy. It was almost too much to believe.

If she'd been superstitious, she'd be real nervous right now. Jenny laughed. Would be real nervous? She could feel her heart quaking in her chest.

Nothing could go wrong now. Nothing. She could practically feel the end in sight. She just prayed that the light at the end of the tunnel wasn't a speeding train.

She made it to his suite and knocked. Bill Hodges, her part-time keeper, opened the door.

"Mr. Todd's in his office. He asked you to go right in."

"Thank you, Bill."

"No problem."

She liked the kid. He was polite, if a little too serious. She wanted to tell him to get out now, but of course, she couldn't. He was still in the hero-worship phase of working for Todd. She'd seen it a lot. Todd was such a persuasive, charismatic man, it was hard for people to believe he was so evil. No one believed it until it was too late. Like a snake charmer, Todd mesmerized his minions and then struck when they were most vulnerable.

If she had a chance, she'd tell Nick to go easy on Bill. And Mrs. Norris. But then Nick already knew about Mrs. Norris. Bless her heart.

Jenny pulled her head out of the clouds as she

walked into Todd's office. He was on the phone, pacing in front of his desk. Across the way, on the conference table, was their lunch. It was an amazing spread of meticulously prepared delicacies, complete with little cards in front of each dish, so they'd know what they were eating. Sautéed foie gras with sour cherries, amaretto polenta and micro greens. Lobster salad with truffle dressing. Vanilla and lemongrass parfait with a rhubarb fruit salad. She'd kill for a Jack in the Box taco.

Instead she sat and took a taste of the foie gras, which, okay, was phenomenal. But still...

"I've got a suite ready for you, Potereiko. Surely you're not going to deny me a chance to play host to such an old friend."

Jenny stilled at the mention of the Ukrainian. This was the second time she'd heard Todd talk with him. As far as she knew, all Potereiko did was sell armaments. Could he be the dealer Nick was looking for?

"Fine, fine. Yes, in public. You have no idea what you're getting yourself into, but fine. You realize there's going to be almost three hundred thousand people here."

She took another bite of something, a tomato, and said a silent prayer that Todd would say where they were meeting. What time.

"I'm sure we will. Yes. I assure you, nothing will go wrong. Until then, comrade."

Jenny sipped her water as Todd hung up the phone. When he turned to her it was with a suspicious eye, but that wasn't unusual. All she had to do was to keep her cool, keep it together.

Todd came over to the table and sat across from her. He ate for a few minutes in silence. Then he cleared his throat. "We'll be married at midnight. In the atrium of The Mystique. Invited guests only. I have someone bringing dresses, in about a half hour. I've been assured the dress will be ready by six tomorrow night. I'll want you and Patrick dressed and ready to go at nine."

"Patrick?"

"He can sleep again once you're at The Mystique. But I want him at the ceremony. I'm going to leave you two there while I go to the implosion. When I finish there, I'll meet you at the atrium. I've planned everything so we'll say our vows at the stroke of midnight, when the fireworks light up the city."

"It sounds wonderful, Todd. We'll be ready."

"Good." Todd took a tape recorder out of his breast pocket, turned it on and dictated for the remainder of lunch. Jenny ate as much as she thought he'd want her too, then waited, wondering what kind of wedding dress Todd would approve of. Something to go with the pink diamond, probably. Gaudy. Expensive beyond belief. It was all so insane.

She needed to tell Nick about the wedding plans. The perfect time for the rescue would be when Todd was at the implosion. She simply wouldn't be there when he came back to The Mystique. Of course, he would probably be in custody by then.

When the designer arrived, she'd had her fill of lunch

and listening to Todd. Not that he talked to her. She just didn't want to hear from him anymore. It was like listening to nails on a chalkboard and being the fawning fiancée was becoming more unbearable by the second.

She eagerly tried on every dress in the batch—all fourteen of them. None of them were over-the-top risqué, which was amazing, and the one Todd chose was actually attractive. White, with pink details, it was a short dress, strapless and, she had to admit, beautiful.

There were also a selection of shoes, all in her size, and he chose the Jimmy Choo sandals with the strappy heel. She wasn't terribly comfortable in them, but that was okay. She wouldn't put them on till she had to.

No veil, thank goodness, and they would have a bouquet for her at the atrium.

In three hours they'd finished and Todd told her to go back to her room to pack. They were going to leave the day after tomorrow. On the fifth. She kissed him on the cheek, he grunted, and she went back to her room. She wasn't at all surprised to see that a matching set of Gucci luggage had been put in her bedroom. How convenient. When the FBI arrived, she'd be all ready to go.

Chapter Fifteen

The meeting was damned inconvenient. Nick had intended to get out of the hotel to meet with Owen about tomorrow. This was the largest bust in the city's history and it would be scrutinized by law enforcement and the media for years to come. There was no room for error. But now was not the time to piss off Todd, so he'd postponed his meeting with Owen and was headed down to the Mogul to meet Henry Sweet and the travel planner to coordinate Todd's departure on the fifth.

He made his way through the happy-hour crowd. Stupid to meet here, but then Sweet liked his afternoon cocktail. Most of the patrons were at the bar, drinking, smoking and playing video poker. Sweet had his usual booth at the back.

Nick checked his watch as he slid in across from Sweet. "Where's Orchid?"

"She's running late."

Nick cursed. "I have things to do."

"Sit tight. She'll be here soon enough."

"Now would be soon enough."

"Have a drink. You could use one."

He grabbed a menu and checked out the lunch specials. "Some of us have schedules to keep. Tomorrow is gonna be a bitch and I don't want anything to go wrong."

"You've got a point. Todd won't be happy if his special day gets screwed up."

"Hey."

Nick looked up to see a man he didn't recognize glaring at him. The smell told him the guy had been having one hell of a happy hour. "Get lost."

"You're the man I came here to see."

"I don't know you, or want to. So just move along, buddy."

The man, who Nick guessed was in his late twenties, was dressed in an off-the-rack suit with a cheap tie, but he was well put together. His hair stuck out in a few places and his speech had that sloppy-drunk feel that would turn quickly into slurred mumbling. He lurched forward, bumping into the table.

Nick stood. "Let's go get you a cab, buddy. You go home and sleep it off." He reached over to grab the guy's arm, but the drunk stepped back. Just as Nick was about to turn and signal the waitress to get security, a fist smashed him on the side of his nose, knocking him to the wall. Pain blossomed as he felt a gush of hot blood on his upper lip. "Son of a bitch!"

He reached for a napkin on the table, but Sweet beat him to it, handing him a white handkerchief.

The blow had been seen by half the bar and security

arrived before Nick had a chance to turn the drunk into paste. They hustled the guy out and Nick heard someone call for a medic.

He sat down, still pressing the handkerchief to his face, and signaled the waitress.

"I'm so sorry, Mr. Mason. Is there anything I can do?"

"Yeah. Bring me a whiskey and a glass of ice."

"Yes, sir."

Nick turned to Sweet. "Great idea, coming here for the meeting."

"What'd you do to that guy? Screw his girlfriend?"

"I've never seen him before in my life."

Sweet grinned. An honest-to-God smile. "Well, he sure as hell acted like he knew you."

"So glad I could entertain you."

"Hey, this was better than a show."

Nick told him where he could put his cocktail, then the medic arrived, carrying a big red box with a big white cross on it.

"Wow, Mr. Mason, what happened?"

"Nothing some time and a few hundred aspirins won't cure. I'm fine. You didn't need to come all the way here."

The medic, Iona, was a nice-looking woman he'd seen often in the employee lounge, although they'd only spoken a few times. "Let me be the judge of that," she said, reaching for the handkerchief.

"I'll take it, if you don't mind," Sweet said. "It was my father's."

Iona got an extra rubber glove and wrapped the stained

cloth before she handed it to Sweet. Then she turned back to Nick. "Doesn't look like he broke anything except the skin. You'll have a bruise, but not a bad one."

Sweet got out of the booth. "I'm gonna go see Orchid myself. I'll let you know later what you need to do."

"Gee, thanks, Henry. You're a pal."

"Glad to oblige," he said, still smirking.

"Bastard," Nick whispered, then let it go. He let Iona do her thing with a butterfly bandage, took the ice pack she offered and stuck it on his face. When the whiskey came, he used it to take four aspirin then, without leaving a tip, he left.

He had to find Owen. Now. He needed to change his instructions about Henry Sweet.

JENNY DECIDED that the only bag she'd take was the overnight case. Heeding Nick's advice, she put all the jewelry Todd had given her in silk pouches, then into the Gucci jewelry bag. She didn't bother with makeup, but she did add some of the creams and shampoos she'd picked up. Who knows where she'd be tomorrow night? Would they send her away immediately to some remote hiding place or take her to FBI headquarters? She wished she could talk to Nick about it.

She'd already decided that meeting him again would be courting trouble. But she had to tell him about Potereiko. She thought writing a note was the best bet, which she could give to Mrs. Norris. The note would also remind Nick to take special care with the nanny. She'd been so kind.

Patrick loved her, and Jenny could understand that. What a stroke of luck that Todd had found her. Maybe, after this, Mrs. Norris would find a nice family to look after. They'd be very lucky.

She went into the bathroom and slowly cataloged her belongings, putting a select few into the overnight case. Her razor, deodorant, things that she might need on her way to who knew where. Then she took virtually everything else and put it in one of the bigger suitcases. The only things she left out were makeup and a few hair supplies. Unsure what time everything was going to come down, she had to be prepared to get dressed for the wedding.

Patrick had been given a little tuxedo for his appearance at the ceremony. She'd seen him in it when she'd stopped by on her way to pack, and he'd looked so adorable.

All she wanted was to have him back. Him and Nick. Her two guys. She didn't give a damn where they lived, as long as it wasn't here.

She'd like to get Patrick a puppy. He was old enough now not to hurt it, and growing up with a dog had been an important part of her life.

As she finished in the bathroom, she wondered what Nick's life had been like. When he'd joined the FBI. Had he always wanted to be in law enforcement? Was Nick even his real name?

It was all so overwhelming. She could only be grateful that Todd was so preoccupied. Hell, he'd been almost human for two days, which was something of a record.

All she had to do was to get through tonight and tomorrow, and that would be then end of it. No one was going to hurt her again. Ever.

She wanted Todd punished for all his sins. She hoped they caught him with the weapon, with enough incriminating evidence to see him in jail for the rest of his life.

What delicious revenge to see him put away with all the other criminals. Having to dress in prison clothes instead of his million-dollar suits. To eat mess-hall food, to have to obey the guards or suffer the consequences. That was almost as good as killing him herself. She wasn't sure she could actually do it, but it wouldn't surprise her. She'd never hated anyone as deeply as she hated Todd.

As if her thoughts conjured it, her phone rang. It was Todd himself, not one of his lackeys.

"I thought we'd have a private dinner tonight. Just the two of us. Be here at eight."

"I'll be there," she said.

She sat on the edge of her bed. He wanted a private dinner on the eve of his wedding. She didn't want to think about what that meant.

He'd been leaving her alone, not making her sleep with him, but her luck might have run out there. It was all right, though. She could bear it one more time. She had to bear it.

Now, however, she'd better write that note to Nick, get it to Mrs. Norris, then finish packing. She had to be on time—or else.

TODD WATCHED as the lab technician worked on the blood samples. He had to type four specimens: his, Jenny's, Patrick's and Nick's. It could be that the blood tests wouldn't give him enough information and then they would have to do DNA testing. That would take some time, but he didn't care. He would do whatever he had to, to determine paternity. On the other hand, this quick test could eliminate him as the father. Or Nick.

He was pretty damn sure that Nick was the boy's father. The birthmark on his back was too similar to the birthmark on the boy, and Todd didn't believe in coincidences.

"How much longer?" he asked.

The tech, someone from Sunrise hospital who did this for a living, looked down at his supplies. "Just a few minutes, Mr. Todd."

Todd nodded. He leaned back, turning his thoughts to the morrow. It was going to be a glorious day. The implosion. Getting the package from Potereiko. He hated to kill the man, but it was necessary. The way he was going to do it was so elegant and simple, there would be no chance of getting caught. One man among three hundred thousand. Who would notice him? After the exchange, Sweet would walk up behind him. The Ukrainian would feel nothing. The injection was being delivered in an air gun, used for vaccinations. It was painless and it would never be heard in all the commotion. He'd be dead in minutes. Sweet would retrieve the money bag and walk away. Simple.

"Mr. Todd? I have the results, sir."

"Go on."

"There's one sample that is eliminated completely from paternity," he said. "That would be Sample A."

Todd smiled.

"That doesn't necessarily mean that Sample B is the father, however. That can only be determined by DNA testing."

"I understand. Thank you for your time. Leave your bill with my secretary."

The tech left the paperwork on the desk and took his bag with him as he left, closing the door behind him.

Todd swiveled in his chair so he could look at his city. He didn't need DNA testing for confirmation. Nick Mason was Patrick's father.

Tomorrow was going to be a spectacular day indeed.

IT WAS LATE and Nick was tired. His nose throbbed again and he hadn't brought any aspirin with him. He hadn't heard from Sweet, but it didn't matter, since Todd would be in federal custody before midnight tomorrow. The meeting with Owen had gone well. The manpower alone was beyond anything he'd been involved with, and he'd been in the FBI for almost nine years.

Nine years. Undercover, this time, for more than three. It was too long. Every book he read about the psychology of undercover operations said one year was too long, two years and most agents were ready for the funny farm. It was too easy to forget what was real. You live in the mud, you can't help but get dirty.

He'd been thinking a lot about that since Jenny had told him he was Patrick's father. Taking Todd down had been his focus for so long, it was almost like a reward, a bonus for a job well done. But was that what he wanted

Patrick to see? It was different when it was just him. Now, though, he had a different kind of responsibility. He wanted Patrick to be proud of him, to grow up thinking his old man was someone strong, right, honest.

He walked slowly down the hall, past Todd's suite to Patrick's. He shouldn't knock, it was nearly eleven-thirty and surely Mrs. Norris was sleeping. There was no question Patrick was in bed. But he knocked anyway.

In a surprisingly short time, the door swung open and Mrs. Norris, still dressed in one of her prim outfits, smiled broadly. "I was hoping it was you."

"Oh?"

She stepped back to let him in. Then she shut the door and locked it. "I had a question, and I thought you might be the one to help."

"I'll do what I can."

"Good. Wait just a moment." She headed back toward her bedroom.

Nick walked around the spacious living room, looking at his son's world. There was a fire truck parked by a stuffed panda, a Patrick-size desk complete with chair and play computer. Action figures, building blocks, plush toys, a telephone, a little piano. It was kid heaven.

Nick would never be able to give Patrick the kind of crap Todd did. He wouldn't be able to hire nannies or nurses, or to send him to fancy prep schools. Once they were a family, Patrick would just be a normal kid. He'd have chores, because Nick knew a sense of responsibility was learned by doing. He'd go to public schools and he'd have to work for the money if he wanted a car.

There would be no silver spoons in his kid's mouth, and Nick had no problem with that. His goal wasn't to raise a tycoon, but a good man. Someone worthy of his mother, which was going to be tough. On the other hand, with Jenny as his mom, how could he go wrong?

"Ah, isn't that a fine fire truck?"

He looked up to see Mrs. Norris enter the room carrying a book. "It's big."

"Patrick loves it. He told me yesterday that when he grows up, he wants to be a fire truck."

Nick cracked up. "I've heard worse goals."

"May I ask," she said, shifting to her right to she could see his nose more clearly, "what happened?"

"I ran into a fist. A strange fist at that."

"Oh, dear. It looks quite painful."

"It is."

"Can I offer you an aspirin?"

"I'd be grateful."

"Here," she said, handing him the book. "I think this is the book we discussed, but I don't understand the passage you told me about. On page thirty-five."

"I'll take a look at it," he said. "My memory isn't what it used to be."

"What is?" she asked. "I'll be back in a moment."

He opened the book, which he'd never heard of, and turned to page thirty-five. A note had been taped to the page. From Jenny.

Todd is meeting a man named Edward Potereiko tomorrow in a public place, my guess is the

Strip near the El Rio. E.P. was at an arms show in
1999 selling weapons from the Ukraine. He's not
a nice man. The wedding is supposed to be at
midnight, at the atrium in The Mystique. He's
leaving us here while he goes to the El Rio. That
would be the best time to find us. Todd will be
busy right up until the implosion, so he must be
meeting E.P. after the implosion, just before he
goes to The Mystique for the wedding.

Also, please make sure to take care of Mrs.
Norris. She's wonderful. Until tomorrow.

He closed the book slowly as he digested the information. Potereiko was the seller, he felt sure of it. He
hadn't heard the name before. It wasn't on any of the lists
from any of the international agencies. But they must
have data on him. He had to get the information to Owen.

Mrs. Norris came back with the pills and a glass of
water. After he took the aspirin, he smiled apologeti-
cally. "I'm gonna have to think about this for a bit.
Nothing's coming to me, sorry."

"It's all right, honestly."

"Actually, I do have some notes I could jot down, if
you have some paper?"

"Right here," she said, going to Patrick's desk. She
picked up a pad of paper and a pen.

Nick wrote as quickly and succinctly as he could, ad-
vising Mrs. Norris that men would be by tomorrow to
get her and Patrick. She should leave immediately, no
questions. She'd be safe and so would the boy.

He handed her the pad. "I've got to go. But if I can, I'll see you tomorrow."

"I feel quite sure of it," she said. "Let me walk you to the door." She put her hand on his arm. As they crossed the room, she whispered, "Thank you, Nick. I appreciate all you're doing."

He nodded, not wanting to risk any more than he had to.

"And for what it's worth, I think Patrick is very lucky to have such a wonderful father."

He stopped to stare at her, but she pulled him along to the door.

"Nannies know these things," she whispered.

"Where on earth did Todd find you?"

She gave her head a small shake. "My sister works for one of his general managers. At his hotel in Monaco."

"He's lucky you were available."

"Thank you, Mr. Mason. I appreciate the compliment."

Then he was in the hallway and the door closed behind him with a click. Something told him Jenny hadn't told Mrs. Norris about him being Patrick's father. That she had in fact just known. Which was a frightening thought, because if she'd known, maybe Todd had known, too.

"ARE YOU EXCITED about tomorrow?"

Jenny smiled at Todd over her glass of champagne. "More than you can imagine."

"My imagination is pretty vivid."

She raised her brows. "I know."

Todd put his glass down. "No, I don't think you do."

His words sent a chill through her, even though they were sitting out on the patio and at eight-thirty, it was almost ninety degrees. "This is the best meal I've ever had, Todd. It's extraordinary."

"I wanted it to be special. You do know I love you. I have since the moment we met. All I've ever wanted is to give you the world on a platter."

"And you have. Don't think I don't appreciate all you've done, Todd. I can hardly imagine my life without you."

"And yet, you ran."

She looked down at her hands. This was no time to be anything but compliant, submissive. "I was a fool."

"Yes, you were."

She raised her gaze. "But that's all over now. I'm here. And tomorrow we're going to be married."

"Yes. Tomorrow we'll take our relationship to the next level. We'll be man and wife."

"Mr. and Mrs. C. Randall Todd."

He smiled and the hair on the back of her neck stood up.

"I've tried to make you happy, Todd. I've done everything I can to prove to you that I'm truly sorry. That I won't do anything so stupid again."

"I know you won't. Are you finished, my love? Do you want coffee? More champagne?"

"No, thank you. I've eaten too much. I need to fit into my wedding dress."

"I'm finished, also," he said, putting his napkin on the table.

The blood in her body froze at the simple words. Something had shifted. His bonhomie had disappeared and in its place there was nothing but ice. Every instinct told her not to look at him, but she must. She had to pretend. To act as if he was simply done with his meal, that his mercurial change hadn't occurred.

Slowly she lifted her eyes. And that's when she knew she hadn't been mistaken. It was like looking into the eyes of hell itself. He knew something. She could only imagine the worst.

"You should go to your room. Sleep. Tomorrow will be a busy day."

As she opened her mouth to acquiesce, the sliding-glass door behind her opened and there stood her watcher. The other one. He was dressed impeccably in a pale blue silk suit. He stood at attention and yet he managed to give off an air of deference in front of the man himself.

Controlling her trembling, Jenny stood. Walked over to Todd's side and kissed his cool cheek. He didn't respond at all. "Good night. I'll see you in the morning."

Todd sipped his coffee, his gaze facing the view, not her. But when she walked to the door, she could feel his eyes on the small of her back. Boring into her. Memorizing his target.

Chapter Sixteen

Jenny woke in her own bed at six o'clock in the morning on the Fourth of July. She'd also been up at four, two-thirty and midnight. She hadn't closed her eyes until eleven forty-five.

Todd had scared her to death last night. The way he'd looked at her. He knew something. Her plan? Nick's involvement? That Patrick wasn't his?

She got up, determined to carry out her part as if nothing at all was wrong. Because this was Todd. And the truth of it was that he could have been that way for something entirely unrelated to her escape. She could have committed any kind of sin and she'd never know until he deigned to tell her. It could have been a look, her tone of voice, something she'd worn.

But she couldn't afford to make one single mistake. Everything in her world was dependent on the success of this operation. Her freedom, her future with Nick. Her son's life.

She went to the bathroom and started a bath, deciding to use some calming salts. Anything she could do to relax was a good thing. Even now, with hours to go, her heart beat so fast she had to be careful not to pass out.

Slipping off her nightgown, she caught sight of herself in the mirror. She looked terrible. Dark circles under her eyes, lines around her mouth, pasty skin. She'd have to take considerable care with her makeup. But first, her bath. Then her hair. Finally the makeup, right before she'd put on the wedding dress. It would take torturous hours, during which she probably wouldn't hear from Nick. She'd have to keep the faith, keep the belief that everything would be all right. What she would do, however, is sneak in to see Patrick as soon as she could. Just seeing him would relax her, at least as much as she could relax under the circumstances.

As she lowered herself into the tub, her gaze caught on her ring. She had no qualms at all about taking it with her and cashing it in. He'd given it to her and she intended to build a bright, shiny new life with the proceeds. However, given the nature of the rescue and flight ahead of her, perhaps wearing it wasn't the best idea. She had no idea where she was going, and flashing this baby around unsavory types might just get her in a whole new arena of trouble.

When she finished bathing, she'd put it somewhere safe. On her body. She'd sew it into her panties. There was a little sewing kit in the top drawer in the bathroom.

After that, she'd go through the rest of the contents in her overnight bag. She didn't want to leave anything important behind.

She laid her head back on the bath pillow and closed

her eyes. Blessed relief came in the form of Nick Mason. She pictured him in exquisite detail, which wasn't hard in the least. She'd dreamed of him for almost three years.

He was so gentle with her. The way he looked into her eyes was almost reverent. It was easy to picture her life with Nick. The mornings filled with the rich scents of coffee and fresh bread. The hustle and bustle of getting Patrick ready for school. Private smiles over the sounds of cartoons. Maybe a little sister for Patrick.

Their nights would be filled with laughter, touching and a peace that would turn the most mundane tasks into miracles. Patrick would grow up healthy. Loved. Encouraged to follow his own path, to find his bliss.

Her new life would begin in a matter of hours. A real life, a real future. It was hard to believe it. For so long the reality of her days was all the colors and textures of fear. She'd been a refugee, a prisoner, a victim. No more. She would sing it from the rooftops. *No more.*

The water had grown cool; it was time to get out, to get on with the day. With her liberation.

NICK HAD GONE through the El Rio with the demolition crew and the reps from the fire department, and everything was a go. There really wasn't any more to do inside the building. They were still putting up chicken wire around the perimeter to prevent any flying debris from getting into the crowd.

The area cordoned off was incredibly tight. He wouldn't have believed it would be safe if he hadn't

seen all the videos of other implosions where the pa-
rameters had been even tighter. These were the experts,
the best in the world, and they had redundancies on their
redundancies.

What Nick was most concerned about, however,
wasn't the destruction of a building, but the destruction
of an empire. Every instinct told him to stop messing
around with this nonsense and get with Owen.

He knew the bomb was in the city, and he'd given
Owen the name of Potereiko, so by now they must have
the rundown on the guy and, just as important, pictures.

They'd identified another potential buyer, a Pakistani, who was holed up in the private suites at the Xanadu. The influx of special agents and support crews had
been going on for days and by this afternoon, everything
should be in place. Command central was at the Mirage.
Once Nick was finished here, that's where he was
headed.

Coordination was everything. No one could afford to
tip off Todd or his men. He hated trusting anyone else to
get Jenny and Patrick to safety, but he had no choice. He
had to get the bomb, get Todd. He couldn't be distracted.

The whole group went out, across the street to where
the detonation would take place. There was a platform
for Todd and the city bigwigs. Next to that, the camera
trucks were already setting up, crews from all over the
world. It was going to be a zoo out here, and that's what
worried Nick. How they were going to spot Potereiko
amid the throngs and, even more critical, how they were
going to take him without civilians getting hurt. It was

a Herculean operation with the potential for a major body count.

The plan was to find Potereiko as he made his way to the meet and to take him and the bomb at the same time they took Todd. The one good thing was that the city streets would be ablaze with lights. The bad thing was that the crowds would be packed together like sardines.

He had to get the hell out of here, over to the Mirage. If at all possible, he wanted to check in on Jenny, at least for a minute, before the games began.

This was gonna be one hell of a Fourth.

JENNY LOOKED at her watch again. It was late, almost eight-thirty. So where were they? She hadn't heard a word, except that Todd expected her to be ready to go at nine.

She had put on the wedding dress. Done her makeup and hair. Even put on some perfume. If Todd stopped by, he wouldn't suspect a thing. He should be gone by now, though. Damn it, where were they?

She checked the little pouch she'd sewed on her panties and, sure enough, the ring was there, safe and sound. Grabbing her overnight bag, she left her room and walked over to see Mrs. Norris and Patrick.

The door opened seconds after she knocked and Mrs. Norris let her in. The nanny's eyes widened as her gaze moved from white wedding dress to Nike running shoes.

"I've got the sandals in here," Jenny said, holding up the suitcase.

"Ah. Well, how practical."

Then there was Patrick, all dressed up in his little black tux. She grinned as he ran on stout little legs to show her how handsome he was.

Mrs. Norris stood by him, smiling like a proud grandma. "He's quite fetching, isn't he?"

"He sure is." She lifted him into her arms. "You're the handsomest boy in the whole world."

"I get to stay up late."

"I know! How lucky you are."

"Can I take my truck?"

"No, honey, not tonight."

"But I need it."

"I know, but you're going to be very busy tonight and we wouldn't want anything to happen to the truck, right?"

"No," Patrick said.

"Yes," Jenny countered.

He frowned extravagantly. Jenny kissed him on the down-turned lips, then looked over at Mrs. Norris. "Is he packed?" she whispered.

Mrs. Norris nodded.

"Are you?"

She nodded again.

"I don't know where they are. It's getting so late."

"Why don't I fix you some tea while we wait?"

"I wish it could be something stronger."

"I have some port."

"No, that's okay. I need to keep a cool head."

"I agree. Now, you two stay clean while I fix up a quick pot."

Jenny took Patrick over to the couch. She let him down, then sank onto the cushion. Her head hurt like the dickens. She had aspirin in her purse and she'd take a couple with the tea. She hoped it was caffeine-free, as her heart was already racing. And she kept finding herself holding her breath.

Patrick was full of energy, running from toy to toy, showing her his treasures. She wished she could take it all with them, but Patrick would get over it. She'd get him new toys, and while they wouldn't be the high-ticket items, he'd have plenty to play with.

Of course, she was going to be very wealthy, herself. She could duplicate Todd's largess. On the other hand, she didn't want to spoil Patrick. She'd ask Nick what he thought.

"See, Mommy? It's a dolphin."

"Wow, what a beauty!"

"He can't go in the water, though."

"No?"

Patrick shook his head. "I took him in the bath and he almost drownded. Mrs. Norris says he has to swim in my 'magination."

"Mrs. Norris is very smart, isn't she?"

Patrick nodded distractedly as he'd caught sight of a Tonka truck. He dropped the dolphin like a used tissue and crouched to play trucker.

"Ah, he's found the trucks."

Jenny looked up as Mrs. Norris brought in a tray with two teacups and a pot with a cozy. Very British.

"I've made Earl Grey," she said, sitting next to Jenny

on the couch. She straightened her plain navy skirt, smoothing it down below her knees.

She reminded Jenny of the queen, although Mrs. Norris was younger. It was the reserve, the bearing. No wonder she'd worked for the royal family.

"Patrick, I have some juice for you."

He dropped the truck and lurched over the dolphin to get at his treat. After he was happily drinking through his bendable straw, the nanny poured two cups of the dark, rich tea.

The amenities, pouring milk, adding sugar, relaxed Jenny more than she would have guessed, although she was still listening hard for sounds of rescue. She'd have liked to talk about it, but there was no reason to throw caution to the wind just yet. Best to just play along and practice patience. She could take a lesson from the supremely calm Mrs. Norris.

She sipped her tea. Slowly. Serenely. She would live through this. All she needed to do was to remember to breathe.

No one, not the CIA, not INS, not Interpol, had a picture of Edward Potereiko. It was as if the man had wiped the Internet clean, made himself invisible. Actually, there was one picture, but his face was obscured to the point of uselessness.

Nick swore again, slammed his hand against the wall of the fifth-floor hotel room that was the communications headquarters for Operation Suitcase. Owen was on two phones at once. There were computers and faxes running on three different tables. Activity was at maximum level.

Nick hadn't made it over to the hotel to check on Jenny and it was damned hard to see how this was going to turn out well. Things kept going wrong. The bomb guys were the worst of it. Their vehicle had been hit broadside by a drunk driver on his way home from Lake Mead. Two of the guys were at the U.M.C. medical center and, while no one was going to die, they weren't going to be defusing bombs, either.

Another team was on its way from California, but that was a delay that could cost them. What he had to do now was to meet Henry Sweet to get the lowdown about tonight. They were meeting at The Mystique, which was catty-corner to the El Rio, just a couple of blocks down.

He checked his watch. He could make up an excuse and run over to the Xanadu, except that the damn streets had wall-to-wall traffic, and what would normally take him five minutes would take an hour he didn't have.

He signaled the assistant director, who was looking older by the minute, that he had to leave.

"Hold on," Owen told him. "Give me a couple of minutes."

Nick nodded. He used the time to get a cup of stale coffee and a doughnut. He couldn't remember the last time he'd had a real meal. Or a good night's sleep.

He sat in one of the folding chairs the team had brought. Four adjoining rooms had been emptied of beds and filled with war-room supplies. No one was allowed on this side of the hotel floor, and there were plain-clothes cops everywhere in this wing of the building.

His gaze went back to A.D. Owen Coffey, his immediate superior for the past five years. He was a hell of a boss and a damn good friend, and he'd been there for Nick during the hardest phases of his undercover life. He'd given him an airtight background, complete with relatives, family pets and school records. No way his cover could have been blown at any time, unless Nick had screwed things up himself. Which he almost had, getting involved with Jenny.

Screw it. She was the only bright light in years of darkness. When he'd taken the assignment, he'd been bucking to become an assistant director. Now, he didn't give a damn about the job. In fact, he didn't want to play anymore.

All he wanted was Jenny and Patrick and a nice, quiet life. He had gone to law school and passed the bar in California, Nevada and New York, but he'd never practiced. He'd been thinking about that a lot lately, in between worrying about the end of the world, and he'd concluded that a nice law practice in some small town where he wouldn't get too many clients sounded real nice.

He wanted someplace quiet, where he could fish, maybe have a little boat. Take his boy with him to catch their limit. He wanted a real community, where neighbors helped each other and the folks at the local store would call him by name.

No more of this. He'd had enough.

"What now?" Owen asked.

"I've got to go meet Henry Sweet. I'll be at the grand-stand by ten-thirty. The building will go down at eleven-thirty and I want Potereiko and Todd in custody by eleven forty-five."

"If we can find a picture of the bastard."

"Find it." Nick stood, finished off the coffee, but left the doughnut on the nightstand. "I'm late. I've got you on Channel Eight. Sweet will be on Channel Four. Got it?"

"Got it." Owen stuck out his hand. "You've done a hell of a job, Nick."

"It's not over yet."

"Don't worry. The good guys are gonna win this round."

"We'd better."

JENNY GOT UP, went to the door, looked out the peep-hole, but all she saw was the wall across the hall.

"Finish your tea, Jenny. It will help, I promise."

She sighed as she walked back to the couch. "You're right. I just can't understand where they are."

"They'll be here. Have faith."

"I do. I truly do, it's just that it's all so frightening. I want so much for it to be over."

"Soon. I promise. It looks like someone has lost a lit-tle steam."

Jenny looked over to see Patrick curled up on the Per-sian rug, his stuffed dolphin tucked under his chin. Sleep had found him, despite his excitement. Good. He needed his rest. It was going to be a terribly busy night. She hoped.

"Tell me something," Mrs. Norris said. "How is it that you ended up with Mr. Todd?"

She took another sip of the sweet, hot tea. "He dazzled me."

"Oh?"

She nodded, still ashamed, still angry at her own foolishness. "I was young and I let the glamour blind me. He can be quite persuasive, you know."

"I do. I've never met anyone quite like him."

"Or," Jenny said, "I imagine, been anywhere like this place."

"No. Never." Mrs. Norris lifted her cup but didn't drink.

A wave of dizziness hit Jenny and she put her tea down, the cup clattering against the saucer. "Whoa."

"Are you all right?"

"Dizzy."

"It's all the excitement. Sit back and breathe deeply. I'm sure it will be fine."

Jenny obeyed, resting her head against the plush cushion of the couch. She closed her eyes, but that made the dizziness worse. "God, I…" She gripped the armrest, trying to stop the world from spinning.

Mrs. Norris stood. "Is there something I can get you?"

"No, I don't…" She cleared her throat, took in a deep breath. But instead of clearing her head, she felt worse. Drunk. Her eyes felt heavy, her tongue thick. "I don't understand," she said, although her voice sounded odd, her words slurred.

"Please believe me, dear. I had no choice."

"Choice?" Her hand slid from the armrest to lie on the couch, heavy as a brick.

"You said yourself he's a very persuasive man. And he threatened the life of my sister. I'm so sorry."

Jenny tried to open her eyes, tried to understand. But she was in a dense fog and the room kept getting darker and darker.

"They're coming now, dear. I hope it all ends up well for you. And that someday you can forgive me."

Jenny tried one last time to sit up. But the blackness was too strong.

Chapter Seventeen

Sweet called just as Nick reached the back entrance of The Mystique. The meeting was going to be held on the forty-fifth floor, in Todd's suite. He hadn't said whether Todd would be there, but it made sense he would be. The El Rio grandstand was a five-minute walk from The Mystique, even with the crowds cramming the streets.

It had taken Nick almost half an hour to go the two blocks from the Mirage, and he'd had to travel the back way, as the police had cordoned off most of Las Vegas Boulevard to vehicular traffic.

As he'd driven, he'd been gratified to see the FBI presence. Teams in cars of all kinds were stationed at every available parking lot, every street that had access to the Strip. He didn't know the agents personally, but he knew the type and he knew the look in their eyes. No way Todd was getting out of here. Neither was the bomb.

He parked, then headed for the elevator, making sure his radio receiver was safe in his vest pocket. It looked exactly like the earphone for his cell phone, so even if it was spotted, it wouldn't raise suspicion. While he was with Sweet and Todd, he was incommunicado with Owen, and he didn't care for that one bit.

All he had to do was to get through today. At the end of it, there was Jenny. And Patrick. Enough of a brass ring in anyone's book.

He felt a certain peace whenever he thought of their future together. It was right. She was right. And together, they were better than either one alone.

But he'd think about that later. He punched the button for the express elevator and it opened immediately. He was alone, which wasn't surprising, as this elevator wasn't available to the public. Only key holders could go up past the fortieth floor.

The ride was swift and he was ready for whatever he had to face. Hell, lying was second nature to him now. Todd believed him to be a loyal subject. There was no reason to start worrying.

At his floor he got out and turned right, heading halfway down the hall. This suite wasn't nearly as grand as the one at the Xanadu, but still it was extraordinarily over-the-top. Five thousand square feet, four bedrooms, six bathrooms. The decor was French Rococo, with ornate furniture covered in damasks and velvets, sheer drapes that pooled on the hardwood floors. The rugs were pastels instead of Persians, but all in all, it just looked expensive as hell.

Sweet was with two men Nick didn't recognize. Todd wasn't in sight.

"What's up?"

"Not much. Waiting for the boss," Sweet said.

Nick, wanting to avoid Sweet before Todd arrived, grabbed an apple on the running board against the wall.

It never got to his mouth.

The pain was like his own private bomb exploding at the back of his head. Then…nothing.

JENNY WOKE on a hard, cold floor, with every part of her body in agony. It was dark, quiet, and she felt terrified.

When she tried to get up, she couldn't move her hands or her feet. It took several panicky moments to realize she'd been bound.

She breathed in, exhaled, over and over until the blind terror passed and she could think. She wasn't dead. Yet. So there was still something to be done. Some way of finding out where she was, how she'd gotten here and how he planned to kill her.

There was, of course, no doubt this was Todd's handiwork. Somehow he'd discovered her plan. She just prayed he hadn't known Nick's part in it.

"Hello?" she said, her voice scratchy and soft. Even that echoed, telling her that wherever she was, it was large. Large and empty and smelling like gasoline.

A garage. That's where she was. In a deserted garage. She rocked, trying to get into a position where she could see more. And where she wasn't lying on a rock. Every move hurt so much. She cried out and in the back of her mind, she kept thinking, *He'll hear me. He'll come.*

When she finally did get to a better position, two things occurred to her. One, the rock she'd been lying on was her engagement ring. And two, that the deserted garage was at the bottom of the El Rio Hotel, which was going to be imploded with her in it.

Not good.

She struggled to her right, her stupid wedding dress offering minimal protection against the harsh concrete floor. Her foot hit something soft.

As her heart sped up, as the fear turned her insides to mush, she struggled to sit up. Patrick, her baby, the one pure thing she'd ever known, was lying in a splash of oil, his black tuxedo jacket hiked up around his middle, his hair flopping over his eyes. He looked as though he was asleep, but she didn't know. If he was…

"Patrick!"

She called his name over and over, the sound echoing off broken and battered columns, huge bundles of dynamite waiting for ignition. She called until she was hoarse, until her tears blanketed her cheeks, dripped off her chin. She called until she saw him move.

And then she just wept. Wept in horror and disbelief that the bastard would do this to an innocent baby. That his cruelty far surpassed anything she could have imagined. He was a monster. And he would burn in hell for eternity for this.

She had to escape. Had to. So she could kill him with her own two hands.

NICK WOKE TO A soft breeze on his face and a gargantuan pain in his skull. He went to rub his head, but his hands wouldn't move. When he opened his eyes, he saw that his arms had been tied to the arms of a Louis XV chair. His legs were also bound, tightly. He struggled against the ropes until he felt his arms burn. When he collapsed back in the chair to catch his breath, he heard the unmistakable sound of Henry Sweet's laughter.

"You can try harder than that, Nick. That was nothing."

"What are you doing, you bastard?"

Sweet walked in front of him, looming tall in the night air. He didn't speak. He let his fist do it for him. He smashed it into the side of Nick's face, crashing the back of his head against the chair, the pain sharp enough to mask his headache, but only for a moment. Soon, he hurt equally front and back.

"Call me that again and I'll slice off your nose," Sweet said.

Nick believed him. "What is this?"

"This? This is the best seat in the house. The best seat in Las Vegas." He stepped to his right, looked out over the balcony.

They were still in Todd's suite. To be more precise, outside his suite, at the edge of his balcony. Nick could see the whole Strip laid out in front of him like a glittering tapestry. From this height, he could see the shapes of thousands of people milling below, but it was too distant to make out any faces. The most prominent thing in his view was the El Rio. So it was before eleven-thirty. "So what?"

"Ah, you don't know. How could you? See, here's the deal." He moved closer, bent forward so his mouth was sickeningly close to Nick's ear. "There's an extra-special surprise in the garage of the El Rio. A package all tightly secured. Two packages, really."

"What the hell are you talking about."

"Your girlfriend, Nick."

Nick's already racing pulse went into overdrive. "What?"

"You heard me. See, your mistake was you forgot who you were dealing with. Todd doesn't miss a trick, don't you know that by now? He knows you screwed her. And he knows the brat isn't his. He's your son. Soon to be your late son."

Nick thrust himself forward, his fury turning his body to fire, his blood to ice. He would kill the bastard maniac Todd. Rip his throat out. But first, he'd kill this son of a bitch.

Sweet straightened, laughing. He took a sip from a tumbler, then walked over to the balcony, blocking Nick's view. He leaned back, took another drink. "You and me, we're gonna watch the building go boom. And then, when the dust settles and the fireworks go off, I'm gonna kill you. I mean, is this a great Fourth of July, or what?"

"I'm gonna send you straight to hell. That's a little kid he's killing. An innocent little baby."

"He's your spawn, Mason, so how could he be innocent? The way I see it is, we're just taking him out before he has a chance to become like you. We're doing the world a favor."

Nick couldn't look at him. He tested the ropes separately, pulling against the bonds he knew were carefully tightened. He had no idea if the two men he'd seen earlier were still here or if they'd gone down to protect Todd. That could have gone either way, but it didn't matter. He had to get out of these ropes, and he had to kill Sweet, and he didn't have much time to do it.

Sweet, looking smug, pulled a cigar out of his breast pocket and took his time lighting it. The smile on his face seemed out of place, mostly because he wasn't a man to smile much. In fact, he was a miserable lout, and it wasn't really a shock to see him enjoying something so macabre. Like Todd, the man had cruel tastes and the wherewithal to see them played out. This, however, was clearly a dream come true.

Nick forced himself to calm down. He'd get nowhere in a rage. He had to think, and he had to be ready to make his move. He'd have one shot at this, and if he blew it, Sweet wouldn't wait. He'd just shoot him between the eyes.

The ropes weren't going to give, not in time. He had no way to get to any kind of weapon. The only thing he did have in his corner was the chair itself. They'd used a dining-room chair. A replica of an antique that, despite its appearance, wasn't all that sturdy. Nick had broken the arm off one about six months ago when he'd bumped into it with a heavy briefcase.

If he could get to his feet, he could smash the chair against the rail. It would break in a heartbeat and then he could get himself out. The problem was how to distract Sweet.

Henry puffed on his Cuban, still leaning cockily against the balcony. His weapon was in his shoulder holster and Nick was sure the safety wasn't engaged.

Just as Nick was about to say something, someone saved him the trouble by setting off a massive firework to the east. It lit the sky with blue and silver, cracked the night with a tremendous boom, and Sweet turned to stare.

Nick stood on the first try, hunched over, barely balanced, and with every bit of strength he had, he swung the entire chair in a curving arc that ended when it made resounding contact with Sweet's back.

The man fell, hard, and Nick wasted no time. He swung the chair again, this time smashing it against the balcony itself, and he felt the splintering of wood as sharp jolts of vibration.

Again, he swung, and this time the right arm separated from the base, and with that new freedom, he was able to maneuver smartly, but he didn't have time to take another whack at the chair. Henry's fist found his chin and Nick went crashing backward, doing more damage to the chair than he ever could have done on his own. He stood again with bits and pieces of chair stuck to his arms and legs, but he was upright.

Sweet went for his gun, but Nick kicked him with the weight of his body behind his foot, and the gun flew out of Sweet's hand through the wrought-iron rail and sailed away into the night.

Growling with fury, Sweet swung at him again, this time connecting with his chest, and the blow knocked the wind out of Nick's lungs.

He didn't fall this time. Instead he wrapped his hand around the length of wood that had once been the leg of the chair, and when he swung back at Sweet, he impaled him in the thigh, blood spurting out, hitting Nick across the chest.

The roar that came from the man was inhuman, but Nick didn't care. He had to get to Jenny and Patrick.

Without a second thought, he charged Sweet, butting him headfirst, pushing him back against the railing. Using strength he didn't know he had, he grabbed the bastard around the hips, lifted him into the air, hardly feeling the blows raining on his back.

With one final burst of energy, he thrust up, carrying the bulk of Henry Sweet like a child. For a long moment they hung suspended, one man lifted by the other, forty-five floors above the city, and then, like a redwood felled in the woods, he went back, back.

Nick let go. He didn't stick around to see where Sweet landed.

"IT'S OKAY, BABY. You don't have to cry. We'll get out of this. I swear."

Jenny prayed she wasn't lying. She'd been struggling forever with the ropes on her hands. She'd had more luck with the ropes on her legs, loosening them enough that she was able stand, but they'd tied her to a column so she couldn't move more than a foot in any direction. Now she pressed harder against the side edge of the column, rubbing up and down, scraping the hell out of her arms, but making no headway with the knots.

If she had to go, she wanted to at least hold him. She'd screamed until she couldn't scream any more. She'd wept, she'd prayed. No one heard. And her baby was crying.

A Klaxon sounded, hugely, painfully loud, and she screamed with the shock of it. Patrick screamed, too, higher, more desperate than ever. He was going to hyperventilate. God, get her out of here!

"Baby, baby, it's okay."

He couldn't hear her. She couldn't hear herself. It was useless, hopeless. No. Never. Not when she had a breath left in her body.

She rubbed against the broken concrete, burning, tearing her flesh, and finally, she felt it. A tear in the rope. It filled her with renewed strength and despite the Klaxons piercing her ears, she worked harder, with everything she had.

Something caught her eye. Movement. She turned, looked... It couldn't be... "Nick!"

"I'm here, Jenny. Oh, God, hang on. Hang on, baby."

He was at her side, and he had a knife, and he was sawing away at the knots, but it wasn't fast enough. She wanted to tell him to get Patrick first, but that wouldn't work because she needed to hold her child.

The Klaxon calls were getting more insistent, the sound of hell itself, and she would go crazy if it didn't stop, if the ropes didn't give...

The rope around her wrists snapped apart and she sobbed as she knelt to help Nick get the last binding free. "Thank you, thank you. Hold on, Patrick, I'm almost there. Nick, hurry, please, please."

Then she was free and she was picking up her baby and hugging him so tight, and they were both crying and crying. Nick tried to take him away, and she pushed him, but he kept screaming, "Listen!" and she heard a new siren, an urgent siren.

She let him take her baby and then they were running, running faster than she ever had, running around the curves of the parking garage until there was the street level.

That's when she heard it, "Ten...nine...eight..." and she ran faster, no room for praying, only for speed. They hit the outside of the structure and Nick grabbed her arm and led her to the right. "Five...four...three..." There was a barricade, metal and sandbags. They had to dive behind it just as she heard, "...two...one..."

The implosion shook the world. She and Nick both hunched over Patrick, covering his body as noise beyond anything she'd ever heard blocked out everything but visions of being inside, being tied, watching her baby die.

It went on and on, dust covering them like blankets, earthquakes battering them with stunning force, between the barricade and the fence behind them.

The visions of her child's death slowly shifted into pictures of Todd. Hate, bigger than the implosion, bigger than the planet, filled her with purpose. She would kill him. She didn't care about consequences. The man had to die. There was no choice.

He'd almost killed her precious child.

"Jenny!"

She opened her eyes, startled that the noise had dulled, the Klaxons stopped. Another noise from behind confused her until she realized it was the crowd, cheering. She sat upright, and Patrick, still crying, but not as hard, struggled to wrap himself around her, to hold so tight she could hardly breathe. God, what a trauma for a baby. Over and over and over, she said, "I'm here, sweetie, and we're safe. I'm here, and we're safe."

Slowly, slowly, she began to believe it herself.

Chapter Eighteen

Edward Potereiko headed south on the Las Vegas Strip. In his right hand he held a lit Bogatyri cigarette, in his left the suitcase nuke, all the way from the Ukraine. Heavy at just over eighty pounds, it would have slowed him down if the streets hadn't been so crowded. It was late, and yet there were children here. What kind of parents would bring children to a place like this? Pressed between all these bodies, not being able to see. Stupid.

He had several blocks to traverse to his designated meeting with Todd. Fortuitously he'd left early with an eye toward strolling and enjoying the glittering street. Now he'd need every minute.

As he passed a woman in a Texas University T-shirt, a man with headphones playing so loud he would surely lose his hearing in a few years, he was overwhelmed with the amount of excess he saw in every direction. The entertainment, the huge LED boards flashing continuous come-ons, the video displays several stories high. And, of course, the hotels themselves. Great, huge buildings, reminding him of Versailles, of the Taj Mahal, of great power and wealth controlled by so few, while millions suffered.

Perhaps the cargo in his suitcase would change things. He was no fool, he understood that if this went off, thousands would die. But thousands died in all revolutions, no? And this thing he carried, the ten-kiloton, uranium-fission bomb was quite capable of killing forty thousand people. Especially if they deployed the bomb in a low-altitude airburst. All they would need was a light aircraft. Flying over the city would not be without complications, but by the time the military were alerted and a fighter jet scrambled, it would be too late.

He, himself, would be far away from any such horror. With the money from Todd, he would resign from political thinking. He would become a nation unto himself, and never again would he have to be part of the machine built to make the rich richer and the poor poorer. He had decided to go to Tahiti. The warmth, the ocean, the tranquil pace. It appealed to him greatly.

He crossed the street, propelled like a pebble in a rushing river. Bumped repeatedly, the Americans typically apologized, the Asians, used to the close body contact, did not. It was all what you were used to. Across from him was Circus Circus in its huge pink dome, which he could just barely see for the dust from the implosion. Soon, there would be fireworks. Soon, he would be a very rich man.

JENNY AND NICK had found an opening in the fence. She held Patrick tightly to her, and his cries abated, although he was still upset. They were all three covered in dust.

"This way," Nick said. "I have to connect with my people. I'll get you and Patrick out of here."

She followed him as they crossed Las Vegas Boulevard, toward Desert Inn. Once they passed the police barricades, the crowd swallowed them whole.

It was madness. She got strange looks, but no one had room to steer clear of them. The short walk took a very long time, and the jostling was upsetting Patrick. She covered him as well as she could with her arms, but it wasn't enough. He needed to be out of here.

"There," Nick said, pointing above the head of a young boy. "That black Taurus."

They fought their way through, each inch a victory. Just before they reached the Taurus, Nick put his arm around her and guided her the last few feet.

The driver, a black man so tall his head touched the top of the car, studied them for a long minute, and then she saw the flash of recognition. "What the hell?"

"It's a long story. I need you to get these two out of here. As fast as you can. They need to be off the street. I need a radio and a weapon and I need it right now."

The driver nodded, leaned over and opened his glove compartment. There was a weapon there, an automatic. He handed it to Nick, along with two clips of ammo. He turned to his partner, a rather stiff-looking woman with short red hair, and asked her for her radio. Somewhat reluctantly, she handed it over.

As Nick holstered the gun, he leaned down once more. "The photo of Potereiko. Do you have it?"

"No. We haven't had any luck."

Nick cursed, banged his hand on the top of the Taurus. Jenny looked at Patrick, at the woman in the car, then back at Nick. "I know what he looks like."

"What?"

"I know. I'll go with you."

"No. Absolutely not. We'll find another way."

"Not in time, you won't." She walked around the car, leaned over. "This is Patrick," she said.

The female FBI agent looked startled, but adjusted quickly. Opening her door, she stepped out and smiled. It transformed her face. "I'm Olivia, Patrick. Nice to meet you."

Patrick buried his head against Jenny's neck.

She hated to do it, but there was no option. "Honey, Olivia is going to take you to get an ice cream. You go with her and Mommy will meet you there real soon."

"No."

"Patrick, sweetie? I have to. You've been so brave tonight. Can you be brave a little while longer?"

His face crumpled into tears and she almost changed her mind. But she couldn't. Someone had to stop these madmen. "I'll be back as soon as I can. I love you. And I'll always be here for you."

He cried in earnest as she handed him over to Olivia. Her gentleness made it a bit easier for Jenny to leave, but not much.

Jenny kissed him once more, then walked away, willing herself not to think of his fear. Not yet. She'd be back and they'd never go through anything like this again.

When she fought her way to Nick, he was on the radio,

talking, searching the crowd. He said something about Fashion Center Drive, which wasn't far. It would be terribly difficult to get there through the crowds and then to spot Potereiko. Like finding a needle in a haystack.

Nick adjusted his earpiece, then took a handkerchief from the driver, Gordon Jenkins, and wiped his face. It was like taking off an inch of pancake makeup. "Take Patrick to the Mirage. We'll find him there. See if you can dig up a doctor to take a look at him, make sure he's okay."

"Will do."

"And get someone else to take your place here."

"It's not going to be easy. The streets are a mess."

"Do it."

"Right."

"We're out of here. Owen knows the drill. You two, be careful."

Gordon turned the key in the ignition. "I was just going to tell you to do the same."

Nick leaned down to see Olivia in the back seat with Patrick. The poor kid was still crying as if his heart would break. "You be good, Patrick. We'll see you soon."

He didn't get a response, and didn't expect one. At least with Patrick safe, he had one less thing to worry about. It burned him that Jenny couldn't go back to the hotel, but she was right. She knew what Potereiko looked liked, and he didn't.

She came to stand next to him, her gaze scanning the crowd nearest them. She'd wiped her face down, too, and looked as though she was about fifteen, and hurting. He touched her arm. "You okay?"

"No. I won't be until this is over. So let's just do it, okay?"

"Here's the drill. You just point him out to me. That's all. And the minute I've got him, you get the hell away. Go to any police officer you see and tell them you need to see Owen Coffey at the Mirage. They'll take care of you."

She nodded. "He's going to be somewhere close. I know they were meeting on the Strip, and Todd isn't going to want to walk far. It's too crowded."

He pointed south, toward the Fashion Show Mall. "Let's go."

They headed deeper into the crowd. Damn, there were so many people. So much potential for things to go bad. Real bad. Yet there was nothing to do but plow through.

He stuck close to her, trying to see, in this mess, anyone carrying a suitcase or a backpack. Which was something of a problem because one hell of a lot of tourists had backpacks. He could eliminate women, men under a certain age, which helped, but still it was nuts. He kept getting bumped, his feet got stepped on. He discovered a mass of bruises he hadn't been aware of.

"I can't see," Jenny said, raising her voice so she could be heard over the cacophony.

He didn't have an answer for her. It would be damn easy for her to miss the guy. Too easy. "Tell me what he looks like."

She paused and someone bumped her from behind. She glared, but it was an older man being pushed himself.

"Jenny."

"Yeah. Okay. He's about your height," she said. "Dark hair, what there was of it, gray at the temples. But that was in ninety-nine."

"Right. What else?"

"He's thin, and he has really prominent cheekbones. He smoked some fancy Russian cigarettes. But all that might have changed."

He repeated her description into his lavalier microphone. Maybe someone would make a connection. At least he knew they weren't looking for a short redhead.

"Good job, honey," he said, practically yelling into her ear. "This way." He took her arm and powered through a pack of elderly women.

On the other side, Jenny paused, staring over the heads of half a dozen Asian tourists. "Follow me," she said a second before she plunged into the middle of the group.

He couldn't do anything else. Except ask God to give them a damn break.

C. Randall Todd smiled with total contentment. The El Rio had gone down in a blaze of glory, taking care of a few personal issues with it. He'd miss Jenny. She'd been a beautiful girl. She'd had no idea how beautiful, but then, that had been part of her charm. He'd find someone new. Someone who understood loyalty.

And by now, Nick Mason was history. He trusted Sweet to dispose of the body in his typical efficient manner. It was time Henry got a bonus. Something sizable. A Lotus perhaps, or a speedboat for the lake. Now there was someone who understood. Not like Mason.

His betrayal hurt worse than Jenny's. He'd treated Nick like a son, and what had he done?

He wouldn't think about that now. He had bigger fish to fry. He'd taken the case with the money from the back of his limo and sent Kahrim back to the Xanadu. The suitcase weighed quite a bit. Not as much as the suitcase he was buying, but it was still considerable. Of course, when he came back, he'd be carrying two suitcases, which is why the meet was to take place so near The Mystique. He never did care for physical labor.

He walked through the crowd, marveling at the sense of anonymity. When was the last time he'd gone unrecognized for so long? Too long ago to remember. He accepted the constant recognition as a small price to pay for all he had. It would be worse after this week. After he turned the bomb over to the authorities.

He could already see the headlines. The tributes. But the real payoff, aside from the millions of dollars he'd add to his coffers, was that the arms community would know exactly what he'd done. They'd understand the finesse, the thought that had gone into his scenario, and the truly important ones would come to him for certain favors.

Which was, of course, the point.

He would be the most powerful man in the world. As destiny decreed.

His hand curled around the injector. Potereiko wouldn't fall for a few minutes. Time enough for Todd to gain a bit of distance, just far enough that when the Ukrainian fell, he'd be able to get the money without at-

tracting attention. Only then would he call out for someone to get an ambulance.

It was such a simple plan. Elegant. Worthy.

JENNY MOVED FORWARD, following the top of a head. It
wasn't much, and it probably wasn't his, but something… There was something familiar about the man…
It could be Potereiko. She tripped over a baby carriage,
but Nick was there to catch her. Not stopping to thank
him, she searched desperately for the head again, and
there it was, in front of a souvenir shop. If she could just
see his face.

Abandoning politeness, she elbowed roughly through
the pack, taking curses as she went. But there, right there,
he turned, looked just past her, and she stopped dead.

Raising her hand, she pointed to him, and Nick, right
next to her, saw him, too.

Nick spoke into his radio, words she didn't listen to.
Her total focus was on the man with the bomb. She
couldn't lose him now. Not after all this.

A moment passed and it seemed as if time slowed.
The crowd, as if sensing the danger in their midst, dis-
persed just enough. Enough for Potereiko's gaze to find
hers. To lock on.

She watched him with fascination. The changes
played on his face. He knew her, but how? Ah. Todd's
girl. The shift of his gaze as he searched for Todd. The
pause as he spotted Nick. The earphone. The gun that
rose above the crowd to point directly at him. His face,
always so reserved, so Slavic in its stoicism, just fell.

He aged a hundred years in half a second. He understood. The game was over.

Nick moved forward and as more and more people saw his weapon, they clawed their way into shops, onto the street, away. "FBI. Hold it right there, Potereiko. Put the case down and raise your hands."

Jenny followed, never moving her gaze from the Ukrainian. Out of the corner of her eye, she saw him bend down. Put the suitcase on the sidewalk. He rose stiffly but not empty-handed. A gun. Gray, big, ugly. It was at his side, moving up, up. "Nick, look out!"

But the gun wasn't pointing at Nick. It moved in a slow arc, up toward Potereiko's head.

Behind him, two men, guns held in two hands, aimed at his back.

"Don't shoot!" Nick yelled at them. "Hold your fire."

Potereiko's gun made it that last inch. The barrel was at his temple.

The FBI men shot him in the back. He went down hard, his own weapon flying from his hand, landing inches from Jenny's foot.

Nick raced over to the body. The two FBI agents were already there. Nick felt for a pulse as the taller of the two men reached for the suitcase.

Within minutes it was four FBI agents, then seven, and the area was miraculously clear, the crowd inching closer already to see.

Jenny bent to pick up the gun. It was heavy. But not too big. She turned right, looking now for another face. Another monster.

TODD HEARD the sirens and turned to look at the commotion across the street. A robbery, perhaps? A murder. Certainly nothing to do with him. Where the hell was Potereiko?

Potereiko would never have betrayed him. He had too much to lose. As for Edward being sloppy? It wasn't possible. He was at the designated meeting place. Potereiko should have been here by now, but if he'd seen the mess over there, he might have reconsidered making the drop. He had Todd's cell phone number. If the plan had changed, he was to call.

Todd shouldered his way to the curb. If he could see what it was…

The corner was swarming with plainclothes cops. He couldn't see past…

Todd froze as a slender woman turned in his direction. He didn't need to see her face to know who it was. But how? How had she escaped? No one escaped when he sent Sweet to kill them. No one. It was impossible.

And yet, as she swiveled and showed him her face, there was no mistaking that it was Jenny. In her wedding dress. She was filthy, but it was her.

He backed away from the curb as he pulled his cell phone out of his pocket. Hitting speed dial number one, he waited for Sweet to pick up, but the phone just rang and rang until an electronic voice told him the party he was trying to reach was not available. Furious, he threw the phone to the pavement and headed toward The Mystique.

There were too many people! He cursed and shoved, not giving a damn who he stepped on. He had to get to his suite. Regroup. Find Sweet. This was his fault. He hadn't tied her up properly. He'd been sloppy. No one gets sloppy if he wants to work for C. Randall Todd.

He glanced behind him. Nothing. But then, to his left. Damn. It was Jenny, and she was moving fast.

He spun around, heading in the other direction.

"JENNY!" Nick yelled.

She didn't turn, didn't acknowledge him at all. She just kept moving. He looked past her, but all he saw were strangers. Except…

Todd. Nick took off after him, cursing the distance between them, the civilians in the way. "Jenny, damn it, stop!"

She didn't.

He crossed the street, but not fast enough to catch her. Todd, who he could only see in bits and snatches, was heading toward Treasure Island. The crowd, impossibly, was thicker there, waiting for the outdoor pirate show.

"Owen, come in." The radio crackled with static.

"Talk to me," Owen said finally.

Nick stumbled over something in the street, caught his balance by grabbing onto a portly man with a video camera at his eye.

"Hey!"

"Sorry."

"What's happening out there?"

Nick regrouped, but kept moving. "I've got Todd.

He's on the southwest corner of Sands. By Treasure Island. Get every man you have over there."

"Roger. Out."

Nick had made inroads, and he was closing in on Jenny. She startled him though, by ducking under a police barricade and edging her way through a long row of teenage girls dressed to kill.

He shouted again. She looked back at him, but didn't wait. Nick could see Todd now, stalled by the jammed crowd in front of the British ship just in front of the hotel. The music started, signaling the start of the show. As Nick watched, Todd climbed over the wooden railing and leaped onto the middle of the ship. He almost fell in the water as he held the grappling rope with only one hand. In the other, he had a death grip on a silver suitcase. As soon as he had his footing, he climbed up the side of the ship, swung the suitcase over the gunwale and clambered over.

There were only so many places he could go. Up the rigging, which was a dead end. Over the side. Onto the facade behind the water.

If he got into the hotel, they were screwed.

Nick pushed harder. He saw Jenny again, making her way through the throng in the middle of the walkway leading to the entrance of the hotel. Nick followed, hoping to stop her before she got in the line of fire. Todd wasn't stupid. He had a weapon, and if he was cornered, he'd shoot to kill.

People were shouting now, being shoved by Jenny, by Nick, who had almost reached her, and some were pointing up to the ship. Nick ducked before a beefy guy with whiskey breath, and when he stood again, Todd had abandoned the ship and made it to the rocks that were the first layer of the elaborate facade that was the staging for the pirate-ship battle.

There were mock stores and cubbyholes filled with pirate treasure, and Todd was having trouble climbing with only the one hand. Nick had to move closer. He couldn't get a shot off with so many people between him and Todd.

Todd stopped, turned his head to look at the crowd. He wavered, climbed another inch. Then he heaved the suitcase as hard as he could, right over the ship and into the water. It hit with a huge splash, and people started clapping.

By this time, the actors for the show were coming on deck. Dressed as pirates, as sailors, they headed for their marks, just as any other night. A few saw Todd, but they still moved into position.

Now that Todd had both hands free, he moved quickly. Damn quickly for a guy almost sixty.

Nick shoved, pushed, barreled his way through people who were literally shoulder to shoulder. He'd been jabbed by so many elbows he'd lost count.

By the time he had made any significant headway, Jenny was almost at the entrance to the hotel. But so was Todd. All he had to do was drop down and run right in.

Nick raised his weapon, but he was too slow. A shot rang out, then another. It was Jenny. She stood in front of an oncoming herd of security men, gun in both hands, getting ready to take another shot. But Todd had his gun out now and it was aimed straight at her.

Nick shouted, but he was too late. Todd's gun went off and Jenny went down.

Nick's heart stopped as he crashed through, but then he saw that it wasn't the gunshot that had felled her, but a security guard, his hands still around her legs where he'd tackled her.

Music blared. That and the special effects were all computerized. Whoever was in the control booth would have no way of knowing about the drama just below his window.

Nick made it to the walkway, near Jenny. He went for his ID, but he didn't have it. All he could do was shout, "FBI. Clear the hell out!"

No one listened. Except Todd. He looked down at Nick, then at the crowd of security just below him. He headed left, toward the pirate ship.

Nick raced to meet him, but in the mass of humanity, he was achingly slow. Todd, unencumbered, moved like a man afraid for his life, and in the next second he'd hit the deck, pushing his way past pirates and their treasure.

Nick tried to get a clear shot, but the actors and stuntmen were all over the deck. "Todd!"

Todd didn't even look at him. He neared the mizzenmast. If he climbed that, he could get to the rocks behind it and, once there, make an easy jump behind the wall, out of sight.

The show had gone on, with the actors' lines booming over the huge speakers set all over the deck. Some of the actors braved ahead, while others stared at Todd, then at Nick. It was close quarters up there, and Todd's gun spoke louder then a megaphone. No one armed with a prop pistol was about to take him on.

"Get down. All of you. Clear the ship."

Some heard Nick and headed for safe ground, but it was so damn loud, and there were so many tourists, that most of the actors were oblivious.

Todd hadn't taken a breather. He was halfway up the mizzenmast, climbing the ropes as if he'd done it his whole life.

Nick ducked under the railing and jumped to some prop boxes in the water. He was finally clear of civilians. Jenny was safe. Todd was going down.

As Nick aimed his weapon, Todd climbed onto the crow's nest. He had his gun in his hand but he didn't aim it at Nick. He turned to his right. Nick followed his field of vision.

Jenny was right there in plain view. Her hands were behind her back, held by a security guard.

Todd pointed his gun at Jenny.

Nick screamed, "Jenny, get down," but didn't wait to see if she obeyed. He took a bead on the center of Todd's chest and fired.

Just as his weapon discharged, a huge explosion made him jump. A wall of fire burst out of the rocks just behind the crow's nest.

As thousands of people watched in horror, the fire engulfed C. Randall Todd, setting him instantly ablaze.

He screamed, once, and then he toppled forward,

slowly, and as he fell to the water below, his flaming body sent sparks flying into the night.

The splash, when he hit, was huge, soaking everyone close to the edge of the water. Nick had to wipe his eyes to see clearly again. To find Jenny.

She was right there, where he'd last seen her. Her gaze fixed on the body, still aflame, white hair floating in the water.

Nick got to her fast, now that the crowd had backed up, away from the danger. He saw an agent he knew nearby and called him over. "Tell the nice security man to let the girl go, would you?"

"Sure thing, Nick."

While they negotiated, Nick moved in front of Jenny. Her gaze, wet with tears, lifted to his. A moment later her hands were freed and she was in his arms. He held her, tight. Rocked her back and forth as their new reality sunk in.

Todd was dead. It was over.

He pulled back just enough so that he could kiss her. And kiss her he did. That very moment, fireworks lit up the sky. In celebration. In gratitude.

They were free.

Epilogue

It was the Fourth of July. Their second since the bad time had ended.

Nick stood in the backyard in his trunks, piling charcoal briquettes into a pyramid in the barbecue. He looked terribly serious, as if one misplaced briquette would ruin everything.

His son, Patrick, stood next to him. Mimicking his dad, he scowled with intensity as he watched every move.

Jenny smiled at her boys. She had all the burgers and dogs ready for the grill, but at the rate they were going it was going to be dinner, not lunch. She didn't mind.

She settled back in her lounge chair, her book forgotten for the moment. Her gaze swept across their backyard, complete with tree house, swimming pool and a pathway that led right to the lake.

Behind her was her dream home. Two stories, plenty of room, a great kitchen and even better family room. They'd indulged in a few places, like the master suite. How she adored her Jacuzzi tub and her magical shower.

But mostly, she loved the house because it was theirs.

Because they'd all been through so much together, and now they had this place in sleepy little Milford, where Patrick had friends and she and Nick were welcomed with open arms.

They'd been married for more than a year, and all of them had worked hard to leave the past where it belonged and to create a family that was strong and supportive and happy.

The amazing thing was that they'd succeeded so well.

"What do you think, Patrick. Ready for the match?"

Patrick nodded. "Good job, Dad."

"Thank you," Nick said, sounding way too much like Elvis. "Thank you very much." Then he took the long lighter and touched the flame to the key spots on the pyramid. He turned to her and grinned. "Half an hour, babe."

"I'm ready when you are."

He walked over, crouched next to her. "How are you feeling?"

"I'm cool."

"Really? No more morning sickness?"

"Not for a week."

"That's a good sign."

"I like to think so."

He kissed her on the nose, then on the lips. Rubbed her cheek with the back of his hand.

"Dad, I want to go swimming."

Nick looked up at her. "Did you hear something?"

"No," she said. "Not a thing."

Patrick stood by the pool, his hands on his hips, his

hair slicked back like his father's. "It was me. Hello. I said, I want to go swimming."

"No one's stopping you," Nick said.

"For real?"

"You've completed your swim classes and graduated with honors. You can go in the pool by yourself, as long as an adult is watching."

He didn't need a second invitation. He hightailed it over to the deep end and jumped in, feet first.

Jenny touched her husband's hand. "He's getting so big."

"I know."

"You think he remembers?"

"I think the bad things fade. He's doing so well in school, and with his friends. I think if there was a problem, we'd see it."

She nodded. "I remember."

Nick winced. "I wish I could take it all away."

"But that's just what you did. You saved me."

"No. We saved each other."

She leaned over and kissed him, then looked him in the eye. "You don't miss it? The FBI?"

"Nope. Not a lick. I like my practice here. Heck, I'm going to be the best damn will writer in Utah."

"You're not bored?"

"Are you kidding? I get to fish six months of the year. What could be boring about that?"

"Sorry. I don't know what I was thinking."

"You pregnant women are all alike."

"Hey, watch it."

He stood, kissing her on the way. "I'm just kidding. No one is like you."

"Damn straight."

"Hey, Dad. Watch this!"

They both watched their son swim the entire length of the pool. When he hopped up, his grin was ear to ear. They applauded, cheering his wondrous accomplishment.

"Like mother, like son."

Jenny looked up at him. "What?"

"I told you once that you were the bravest person I've ever met. The strongest."

"And?"

"And Patrick is just like you. He puts his heart into everything. He's brave and determined and he does his best, always."

"And you don't think he got any of those traits from his father?"

"Nah. All he got from me was dark hair and flat feet."

"No. You're wrong. He got something else."

His hand rested on her shoulder. "What's that?"

She held out her hands, about a foot apart. "He's got a *huge*—"

"Jenny!"

"Heart."

"Ah."

She smiled. "Ah, indeed."

Nick headed for the pool, but stopped just before he reached the deck. "Did I tell you I loved you today?"

"Several times."

"Just checking." Then he ran to the deep end and jumped into the pool, feet first.

Jenny sighed. This was so much better than her dreams.

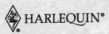
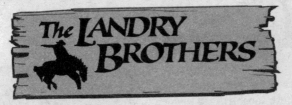

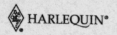

If you enjoyed what you just read,
then we've got an offer you can't resist!

Take 2 bestselling love stories FREE!

Plus get a FREE surprise gift!

BRINGS YOU THE THIRD
POWERFUL NOVEL IN

LINDSAY
McKENNA's
SERIES

Sisters of the Ark:
Driven by a dream of legendary powers,
these Native American women have
sworn to protect all that their people
hold dear.

WILD WOMAN

by *USA TODAY* bestselling author
Lindsay McKenna

Available April 2005
Silhouette Bombshell #37

Available at your favorite retail outlet.

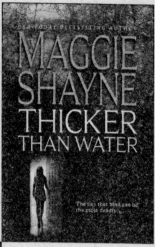

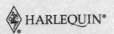

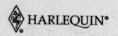 HARLEQUIN®

INTRIGUE

Has a brand-new trilogy
to keep you
on the edge of your seat!

Better than all the rest...

THE ENFORCERS

BY DEBRA WEBB

JOHN DOE ON HER DOORSTEP
April

EXECUTIVE BODYGUARD
May

MAN OF HER DREAMS
June

Available wherever Harlequin Books are sold.

www.eHarlequin.com

HIEB